Scars of the Prophet

Mingo Kane

Copyright

Author Website: `http://mingokane.com`

ISBN-13: 978-1484000694

ISBN-10: 1484000692

Dedication

This book is dedicated to all the men and women who have served this country in the U.S. Armed Forces. To those who have suffered from PTSD and still suffer today. Thank you for your sacrifice. You are always remembered.

PART One: Coming Home

"The deadliest weapon in the world is a marine and his rifle. It is your killer instinct which must be harnessed if you expect to survive in combat. Your rifle is only a tool. It is a hard heart that kills. If your killer instincts are not clean and strong, you will hesitate at the moment of truth. You will not kill. You will become dead marines and then you will be in a world of shit because marines are not allowed to die without permission. Do you maggots understand?" Gunnery Sergeant Hartman
- Full Metal Jacket

Sergeant Johnson told me the day I was discharged after my third and final combat tour: *'Pain is a weakness of the mind that eventually exits the body.'* I'd had my fill of his ribald Marine bravado; there had to be a moral divide. Pain was pain. Pain endured.

I shook those memories free and boarded my plane that was bound from Los Angeles to Las Vegas. It was just another day in paradise.

I gave up my window seat to a googly-eyed kid from some Kansas hick town. His sister argued that she had asked me first while trying to wedge herself into the seat between us. The hayseed kid and his sister kept bickering over who called the window seat first and it was pissing me off.

Instead of telling them to tone it down, I plugged into my iPod before they could draw me into their personal squabble and let the tone-deaf music and subtle vibrations of the pre-flight logistics entice my heavy half-lidded eyes. I hadn't slept more than a few thirty-minute catnaps during the past week of travel and rigid Marine ceremony, and I reclined back to grab a few winks. Maybe it would get me back to feeling good. Not great or wonderful—those days were remnants of another lifetime and a far away place that was lost to me forever. The sinew of it all had me stretched taut to where every day good was as normal as it got.

I looked at the pop-eyed kid's ears and remembered a young Marine I had served with in Iraq. I nodded off as the runway lights sped forward and my subconscious world faded back to a conceived time born from the blood of violent young men.

He was a tan California surfer dude who rode bone crushing waves as big as his ego. It seemed as though the government had snatched Jeff Spicoli from Ridgemont High, handed him a rifle, turned him into a killer, and transplanted him in Iraq. His ears stood out well past his head like curled orange peels left to dry in the sun. Because of his red hair, Sergeant Johnson dubbed him 'Bozo' in a platoon where everyone answered to single word identifiers; 'combat-names' in our happy band of Iraqi killing prophets. Johnson stayed on Bozo's ass and used those enormous head flaps to bring out the madness we all fought to control.

"Goddammit Bozo, get your fucking k-pot on and cover those damn ears before you set off an IED with those floppy bastards. I swear to God, those fucking ears of yours look like air brakes on a buzzard's ass," Johnson would yell.

The last time I saw the kid, Frag and I were pulling security while the medics loaded Bozo into the back of a Humvee. His arm had been blown off from the elbow down as if some arcane animal snatched it off with one cauterizing bite. He held the bloody and blackened stump to his face and kept screaming over and over:

"You can't surf with one fucking arm!"

Frag and I waited for the Hummer to wheel Bozo off and took turns spitting our tobacco juice on a gathering mass of sand ants feasting on the microscopic remnants of his detached limb. Frag bent and took the wristwatch off the severed hand, held the bloody time piece to his ear to make sure it was still ticking and then looked at me with those blank and insipid eyes. "I'll tell you one thing... you gotta admit ole Bozo's got a point."

"What's that?" I asked.

"A one armed surfer's just gonna paddle his board in a fucking circle." Frag said it casual, like he'd off-handedly solved some quirky riddle.

A hand grabbed my shoulder, causing me to snap awake with my fists clenched ready to strike. The girl threw her arms to her face to block the impending punch. "Your eyes were wide open but I think you were having some kind of bad dream, mister," she said and lowered her hands slightly. "Sorry to scare ya like that but you were spazing pretty bad and about to fall out of your seat."

Her bug-eyed brother leaned in and grinned like a mad scientist. "Damn, dude, I thought you were fixing to deck Jenna."

"I'm sorry, flying doesn't agree with me," I apologized, getting out of my seat and going towards the rear of the plane.

The other passengers were watching me as I walked the aisle to the lavatory. I stepped inside and locked the door then scrubbed my hands under hot water until they were pink and puffy. The scalding water felt good on my hands, like scraping butchered hogs on crisp fall days. I looked into the mirror with Bozo's memory branding the reflection.

I gagged and dropped to my knees, puking; the metal toilet felt cold and comforting like a falsely constructed idol. I liked this Hunter S. Thompson world of mine. I was an old and faithful customer to this unwritten gonzo realm of decadence. I made a bad decision after my first tour when I plucked heroin from the forbidden tree and lost sight of Eden to that illicit fruit. I stayed in an ancient world where the pulse of my life stagnated for three months. The bee sting prick as spoon-heated liquid plunged into vile and diabolical veins, carried away to a land of the landless where agony sprang from epicanthic eyes with fiendish delight. I swam in that Pink Floyd incantation where comfortably numb befitted the junkie king and another brick lay freshly mortared in the prehistoric wall of purple hazed visions. It took me seven months to get clean enough to pass the drug test so I could reenlist for a second tour of duty in Iraq.

A set of knuckles rapped the door, "Are you alright in there, sir?"

"Yeah, just a little queasy from the flight," I lied and opened the door to a frowning flight attendant.

"Can I get you anything? Maybe a club soda?" she asked in a medicinal tone.

"No I'm fine now. Thank you." I spotted an empty seat near the front of the plane and asked, "Ma'am, I don't want to disrupt the other passengers so do you think it would be alright if I sat more towards the back of the plane until we land?

She looked at the medals and ribbons on my dress blue uniform and gave me a wink. I liked that wink. "We're really not supposed to allow it but it's only an hour or so until we touch down. Go ahead and if anyone asks just tell them Tammy said it's alright."

"Thank you, Tammy," I answered and moved towards the vacant seat while purposely avoiding the bumpkin girl and her brother's oafish stare as I passed by their section.

I pulled the blanket over my head and left a peephole so I could stare out the plane's window. Anyone who passed by would see my covered back and think I was asleep, but I knew different. You learn to hide from that part of the disease and compensate by obviating solitude and staying awake. It's the perverted side of war soldiers won't talk about because they can't, it stains you like an invisible tattoo and covers the core of what you once were, hiding it forever.

I came back after my first tour of duty to a foreclosed home, as well as friends and a soon to be ex-wife who thought they understood the enormity of the scars. "*Man if I was over there with you I'd fucking kill every camel-humper I saw.*" One of my all-time favorite beer courage rants from redneck friends too chicken shit to actually fight anyone other than their wives.

No you wouldn't, tough guy. Once the liquid muscle wore off you'd be scared like I was scared. You'd throw yourself to the floor of a Humvee like I did with your fucking eyes clenched shut while praying from a fetal position that you wouldn't hit any IED's. You'd be face down in the sand shitting your pants like I was, hoping you wouldn't get hit during a firefight while hearing the screams from friends and trying to put a face to those calling out for the medic. Crimson sand and the blackened craters of broken dreams become your new reality and I saw enough reality to last an eternity.

The real truth abides once the filming stops and the fighting isn't newsworthy anymore. It's the dark part of war that Fox and CNN can't capture - what really lurks behind the young warriors' brave eyes.

What about the never-ending screams coming from the wounded? They're lost to the anchorman's monotone voice giving the viewers at home an updated causality count. There's no drug to silence those screams and they will echo with unchanging clarity in the chambers of your psyche forever.

Those black rings encrusting your nostrils from the stringy tendrils of burning rubber? They're not Pulitzer worthy, so the cameraman decided to film the dead kid's milky and varnished eyes. That odor of burning rubber mixed with cordite burns in the mind long after they're extinguished in the here and now.

Those sudden cracks of gunfire coming from who-the-fuck-knows where? The microphone was off so they cut to a beer commercial. Pops and backfires become the devil's bark and those memories obey no one.

The ordered courage of men kicking in doors trying to find the shooters? They're shared by the soldiers inside and won't make the four o'clock edit back home. You open and close a lot of doors over there and what happens behind them evolves into a war that you will fight until you breathe your last.

You see it every fucking day until you become trapped in that fog of war where every man fights his own private battles. That place where you're always shooting at shadows. That place where demons are real and your deepest fear is that you have become what you are fighting.

You come home to structure and try to leave *that* part of you where it belongs, that passion for the honest and brutal savagery of violence - but you can't. Not ever. There is no exorcism for those demons now within you and they speak to you and they do not lie. You become a prisoner to the truth, shackled to dark shadows and darker dreams while the rest of the world passes you by.

It was my mother who finally convinced me to attend a veteran's support group after my first tour was over. I hated them. I went to three meetings where I sat semi-circled among half-stumped soldiers with the same dull and lifeless eyes. We were fed little blue pills for their false dominance and their sweet taste of nothing and became invisible men with missing lives that learned to walk on little blue-pill crutches. In time, we dealt with our demons the same way, alone.

"What are the flashbacks like?" the counselors had asked.

"Like waking up from a nightmare when you were never asleep," I told them. You stayed awake to keep your demons in the night world and you never showed weakness. Weakness allowed them to haunt the world of the living.

They said at the VA hospital that total recovery could take years. I didn't have years and the counselors couldn't understand that. The pills started a week later. *"Consider each pill you take as a way of shaving a month off your total recuperation time,"* they said. I took a lot of pills and they put me in a world of light and dark. Get up, eat, sleep, light and dark... nothing else. I couldn't live like that anymore. A month later, I was deemed mentally fit and back in Iraq for a second thirteen-month combat tour.

The plane touched down with a lurch, pushing those thoughts back where they belonged, buried and hidden among the once forgotten. I rubbed my eyes to erase the mechanical buzz of sterile voices filing into the aisle with yawns of false patience. Hiding impatience on your face is like hiding the fact that you have to piss. It's that pinched smile airline passengers always give you while they wait for their turn to duck into the aisle and offload the plane. Their greedy way of letting you know they're next. Pinched piss-faces waiting for the shuffling line and the warm voice telling each flyer, *"Welcome to Las Vegas, and remember...*

What happens in Vegas stays in Vegas." The world would be a better place if what happened in war stayed in a war.

I filed through the terminal and picked up my duffel bag at the carousel, three handshakes and a dozen questions about my uniform and medals later, I found an empty seat and waited for my connecting flight to Charlottesville, Virginia. A young blonde sat across from me and smiled, no small talk, just a friendly smile before she shoved her nose into a book and I disappeared back to the world of ordinary… but I was anything but ordinary. My head tilted to my chest and I wanted to doze, but I knew better; sleep brought the demons and I wasn't going to chance that in a public place. When I came to Sergeant Johnson's platoon, he instructed each one of us to yoke one arm behind our backs so we wouldn't sleep on watch. Like being handcuffed, the arm would cramp after thirty minutes and force the mind to stay awake. Insomnia was better than sleep. The dead only lived when you slept and I no longer controlled that part of my existence.

They gave us thirty days leave once we finished that first thirteen-month tour and had become full-fledged killers for democracy's cause. Thirty days to decide if we had had enough or if you still craved their brand of egomaniacal bloodlust. I spent the days at home with my wife and parents trying to hide my eagerness at getting back. I didn't feel like this was home. I needed to be among those like me, those who understood and followed the new rules, the ones issued by the Marine

Corps. I had made my choice to reenlist a second time before my feet touched American soil and before my wife had asked me for a divorce.

Mom took me to church to pray the day I left. It was a Monday morning and the groundskeeper had just finished mowing the lawn. It was the last time I would ever smell fresh cut May grass. After that, the only odors I could recognize with absolute clarity were that of burning rubber and cordite. We sat in the pew beside the cages where raspy skin grated to the buzz of snaky rattles. George Went Hensley left the Church of God in Cleveland, Tennessee when they found out he was handling poisonous snakes. It wasn't long before sister-churches sprang up throughout the Appalachian backwoods around the turn of the century where the practice caught on. Handle deadly vipers, partake of poison, talk in tongues, and receive total submergence in water to receive the Holy Spirit. It was the Appalachian backwoods, Pentecostal way of getting into Heaven.

Mom looked at me and smiled. "They're restless and rattling today, ain't they?" she said with a nod toward the cages.

"Naw, Momma, they were just napping and we spooked them when we came in."

She leaned close to my ear and whispered, "Recite from the book of Mark, chapter 16: verses 17 and 18."

"And these signs shall follow them that believe. In my name shall they cast out demons and they shall speak with new tongues. They shall

take up serpents and if they drink any deadly thing, it shall not hurt them. They shall lay hands on the sick, and they shall recover," I answered and gave her Luke 10:19 to recite.

"Behold, I give unto you power to tread on serpents and scorpions, and over all the power of the enemy and nothing shall by any means hurt you," she replied. We sat there in the pew with eyes closed and prayed through the scaly rattle of snakes. "Don't ever forget this, Tom," she whispered, "I want you to think of going back over there like you're a prophet of the word and you're taking God back home to the holy land."

I answered with: "And I saw heaven opened, and behold a white horse and the Prophet that sat upon him was called Faithful and True, and in righteousness he doth judge and make war. His eyes were as a flame of fire, and on his head were many crowns and he had a name written, that no man knew, but he himself. And he was clothed with a vesture dipped in blood, and his name is called The Word of God."

"Revelations," she said, "and Exodus 20:13?"

"Thou shalt not kill," I replied.

"Thou shall not murder," she corrected. "The taking of a life has never been prohibited in the Bible. What is prohibited is the taking of innocent life, that is, murder. You do what you must to stay alive and come home to us, Tommy. God forgives the killers in war. He just ain't gonna forgive the murderers. They'll be judged differently when they stand before Him. Remember that, son."

"Promise?" I asked.

"I give you my wink of love on it," she winked at me then closed her eyes and prayed.

I awoke sweating to the unsanitary sanity of that dream; mother was gone and so was my connecting flight. I had zoned out again. We called it 'droning' in Iraq. Your eyes were open and you were fully conscious, but mentally you were in another world and it was happening to me more and more often. They had sent me home too soon, I wasn't ready for that and home wasn't ready for me. It was never about the brutality of war—it was a gravity of consequences and what that fraudulent violence had left behind. I still felt hollow inside, like I had exposed a raw nerve to some sinister presence. My mind wouldn't let me leave Iraq and I still lived where devil dogs ruled the testosterone-driven hell of Hemingway's alpha-male world.

It's the ugly side of Post Traumatic Stress Disorder no one talks about, that passion for the most ancient of human appetites—violence. I went off to war with God as my protector and guide, then came home expecting Jesus to take me back after my final tour. That's when the thrice nailed prophet laughed down from his perch and gave me a new set of rules to follow.

PART Two: Sinners Without Sorrows

Las Vegas

"I'd rather laugh with the sinners than cry with the saints. The sinners are much more fun You know that only the good die young."

Billy Joel

I cashed in my airline ticket and hopped a cab from the airport to the Vegas strip where the neon haze lit the desert wasteland like an obscene cruise ship without water. The sidewalk was littered with the lesser fools in life, moving about the filth yelling and peddling forbidden wares that ranged from female flesh to drugs. I got a room at the Days Inn just off the main Sin City drag and sat in a chair watching the slimy world through my peepshow window, it becomes a habit and you cannot explain the reason why.

You never notice the changes. They grow inside you and become defining traits and yet your view of the world hasn't seemed to change. They mark you and those scars are eternal. The people that are closest to you are the first ones who will look at you differently. You catch their frugal glances when they think you are not watching. But that's just it, you are always watching. It has become you and it will always be.

When you go to a restaurant, you find the table in the corner, close to the back exit. You seek this spot out without thought or reason, but from that position, you can see everyone that comes and goes. It's never a conscious act; it is a validity that just happens.

When you enter or exit a building, even your own home, you give a quick scan to secure the area. Your wife asks you if you forgot something when you do your little security sweep. All you reply is, "Nope" because you can't explain it yourself. It's automatic. It's embarrassing.

You find yourself checking locked doors a second or even a third time. You look at familiar surroundings as if for the first time. Common sounds that you've never noticed before give you pause: Deaf ticks of a clock in a lifeless room, bumps and thumps alert you and put you on instant guard. You are a child again experiencing the world for the first time and yet you have aged beyond your years.

You never take the same route on consecutive days, even to daily destinations. Your commute to work, your trip to a friend's or relative's house seem meandering and if someone is with you and asks why you are going a different way, you shrug and say, "I was day dreaming" as you survey the rear-view mirror while honestly believing your own excuses. But they are all bullshit. You can even fool yourself sometimes. Until a smell or a face or a feeling brings it all back and you remember the things that have forged the new you and you feel the tightness in your chest because you want the old you back. Even for an instant— just one fleeting moment of peace. Just one.

You want the old security. You want the old innocence. You look into a mirror and sometimes don't quite recognize the stranger looking back and you wonder when it changed as if it were a single event or incident that brought about this transformation.

You never answer the phone on the first ring and whenever it does ring, it startles you.

You look everyone in the eyes, but it's more than just being polite. It's probing, looking for a change, misdirection, some dark and hidden deceit. People can't help but break eye contact with you because at some instinctual level, they feel you are dangerous. And you are.

You never answer the doorbell immediately. You always check the entrance from a different location first.

You can no longer stand to be in crowds for any length of time because you see everyone as a threat. You never walk around corners without 'slicing the pie' and checking all quadrants.

You are always armed because you have become a weapon.

You miss counting or depending on others because you cannot surrender or place your security in anyone else's hands. Riding as a passenger in a car becomes uncomfortable and an almost unbearable loss of control, and the one thing you will miss most of all is the honest province of laughter.

I sat watching the world pass by beneath the smoke and the haze and let my own world drone away...

The first time I saw Sergeant Johnson was during our initial in-country briefing once we arrived in Iraq. The Chaplain had a small service going for Danko, Pitman and myself when Johnson pushed the doors open.

"Where's my fucking cherries?" he asked.

The Chaplain winced. "I will be finished with my service in a moment, Sergeant. Allow me to conclude the benediction and they are all yours."

"That's fine, sir. Nothing like a little dose of Jesus Christ to start the day off on a good note." Sergeant Johnson looked at us and winked. I liked that wink. Confident.

The Chaplain nodded. "Let us bow our heads saying amen: Blessing, and glory, and wisdom, and thanksgiving, and honor, and power, and might, be unto our God for ever and ever. Amen."

"Amen," we answered.

"Is that it?" Johnson grinned, shrugging his shoulders. He was the most squared away Marine I had ever seen and there on his dress khakis, sitting atop a cluster of ribbons, was the unmistakable blue and white of the Navy Cross. This was a Marine, a professional warrior and a true prophet of ruin.

The Chaplain had about lost his patience. "Sergeant, I can understand that you may not look at this war from my standpoint, but I am here to offer something better to those who may not return home."

"What's the offer, sir? Hell, if it's better than what I got I may take you up on it," Johnson grinned.

The Chaplain sighed. "I offer paradise."

"Paradise, huh?" Johnson smiled, walking closer to the Chaplain. "Sir, let me advise you about my vision of paradise. Every day that I stand in the door of a Blackhawk helicopter and look down at the smoldering ruins of Baghdad, I see my paradise. When I feel the ground shudder from another bunker buster burying a dozen sand niggers in some shithole they call home, I hear my paradise calling. Each time I send another one of these fucking sandal-wearing demons on an expedited trip to Allah, I'm in my paradise." Johnson lit a cigarette and looked at our faces. "And today, well, gentlemen, today is just another fucking day in my paradise."

"Is that it? Is that what you believe in your heart, Sergeant?" the Chaplain asked.

"My vision of paradise preserves your right to preach about yours. We'll see what these fine young prophets believe after they spend thirteen months in this sandy shit box." Johnson took a drag off his cigarette and exhaled. "We'll see what choice they've made then, sir… follow you to your paradise or follow me and create mine."

I showered and changed from my military uniform into civilian clothes before stepping out to greet the nighttime world of sinners and saints alike. The pounding beat of techno music cut the exhaust laden air and pulled me toward the sound as if some maddened piper had now beckoned my unworthy company. The club was a leather walled miasma of fog where lasers split the slimy air like devilish fingers seeking craved and cowardly flesh, chem-lite warriors spun in dancing arcs to synthesized rhythms like revelers or conjurers practicing some ancient craft. The bouncers moved through the crowd with shaved heads and gold hoops in their ears, comic louts that used their brutish size to dictate the rules of their newfound world. I was like them once upon a time, sharing in laughs and lies where oblique shadows and pale reflections illuminated the young lords reining supreme over their night time world of excess. And the nights were always excessive for me.

When I came home after my second tour, I tried to fit back in but couldn't hold a regular job for more than a couple of weeks. The failed careers began with a union welding gig and ended as a police officer when a night of weakness showed up on a drug test. I smoked one joint to kill the nightmares and, from my parent's point of view, *"I would be branded a drug dealer for the rest of my life"*.

They perked in the way that honest parents do when I used my military benefits and applied to a few colleges. I got a kick out of their 'God has answered our prayers' vision of redemption, our son the doctor or *my* son the lawyer. The disinfected dream all parents have for their children; grow up and become doctors or lawyers—one the good guys.

It's a status thing among backwoods Appalachian communities when the gossiping buzzard whores gather to one up each other through their double-wide dwelling, meth-addicted children. I shattered my parents lofty dreams by majoring in journalism but dropped that and James Madison University after two semesters of fights, drugs, and threatening the faculty. I saved face for my mother's sake and enrolled in a creative writing class at a local community college. If you can't focus, you can't write. I quit that course after thirteen sessions.

I finally took a gig as a bouncer working the all-night raves and topless clubs on weekends for extra money. It wasn't much, but it was the job of jobs for someone like me; plenty of booze, drugs, and late nights with no sleep. And the violence was always there in tidbits—just enough to whet the appetite like a junkie who needs 'just enough' to get by. I thought life was finally taking an upward swing. I was playing by their rules. I had found a home built on compromise and truly believed that I had found a niche where I could merge what I once was with what I had now become. But it was never enough and the fights became more frequent until I almost beat a man to death for slapping his wife. The judge took my military service into consideration and gave me two options: serve a year in jail for aggravated assault or reenlist and spend another year in Iraq. Jesus endured three nails and a cross for the sins of this world and I endured three tours of combat in a war without consent.

I pushed those thoughts away and watched a blonde chick rule the twisted world of three guys who worshiped and encouraged her drunken moves with lusty grins. The men were the divorced-and-twenty-years-past-their-prime crowd with shitty do-it-yourself dyed hair. The girl looked at me and smiled; I'd seen her type in the clubs where I had bounced. She craved the attention her looks could bring without the bullshit diatribe and she was just trashy enough for sexy.

"Where you from?" she asked, sloshing her drink over a sticky sunburned arm.

"Virginia… You?" I didn't like her waxed eyebrows or her tic-tac smile.

"California *bay-bee*." She held her drink in the air and screeched out the last word like a Cancun spring breaker.

I ordered straight scotch over ice to take the edge off and hoped it would ease me into a better mood—instead of this—but I wanted her company. I didn't want to be alone. Not now.

"I'm Cammie," she yelled above the music.

"*Carrie?*" I asked, not sure what she'd said.

"No, not Carrie, I'm Cammie."

"I'm Tom Judah."

"You wanna dance?" she asked, sliding her tongue around the straw, teasing the implement before taking a sip. Her tongue was pieced. A shiny metallic ball clinking against her conch shell teeth, luring me in with its reason for being there—blowjobs. I thought about how it would feel as it slid up and down my shaft, goading the head in tight circles before her wet mouth dropped downward in gurgling spasms.

It was so easy for me to fall into her temptation and the normal-guy image she sought only fueled it. I knew where this situation was heading and I could've easily walked away but I didn't. I had her hooked with the vision she wanted and she had me snared with the fantasy I'd created.

After two hours of dancing and lies about exotic travels over drinks of seduction and come-ons, we stumbled back to my hotel room. Her tongue had the residual taste of piña colada on that pierced and foreign orb; our legs intertwined and writhing in that groping pre-sex struggle, thong pulled aside revealing the fresh shaved pubic stubble and a wetness like a slick and peeled peach leaving its mark on probing fingers. I liked how easy Cammie was, just bait her with the mechanics of lust disguised as pledges of love. It wasn't her first time and the truth of this lay behind a Gorgon's mask that covered her intentions. But I could feel the pains of guilt and shame welling up from within that dark and cavernous reach inside me. Things were different with me now. My outlook on life had changed.

"I can't do this," I lied, hoping she'd get the message and return to her previous audience. I had found that I could only take companionship in small, measured doses these days.

"That's no fair." She sat up and pouted her lips trying to be cute and perky.

I wanted her to leave and resented that childish pout, but I wanted it to be her choice without me having to tell her to split. Cammie seemed determined to hang around by trapping me with her small talk. It was that idle bad girl chatter and I really wasn't interested in her problems or how her friend couldn't meet any nice guys in Vegas. I had demons of my own to struggle with and I didn't need her extra ruck.

"It's almost midnight and a big party is just starting up at the Bellagio. I can find my girlfriend Sarah and we can grab a quick bite to eat and hang out a little more." Cammie's voice almost pleaded for the extra company. "If you want to..."

The thought of getting two girls drunk enough for a threesome gave me a host of greedy self serving thoughts Charles Bukowski would have envied. I knew it was a bad decision and bad decisions had recently defined my life. Something Sergeant Johnson had said to the entire platoon rang back through time like some distant voice of prophesy:

"Bad decisions will breed a conscious so you men may as well face those facts, because sooner or later, you're gonna make a mistake. I've got no time in my platoon for men who make bad decisions or worry about what choice their conscious tells them to make. I need men who will react without hesitation when the time comes and worry about their conscious once they get back home. You men are trained killers and every fucking one of you is going to become a personal prophet of ruin to these Iraqi sand demons."

"Maybe some other time," I said, feigning a yawn. "I've got to get up early and leave in the morning."

"Are you sure? I'll make it worth your time if you stay," she teased in a voice that betrayed her coy appetite for romance novel fantasies.

"I'm sure, I've really got to get cleaned up. I need to stay clean both inside and out."

"No biggie... but it's your loss," she said gathering her things and stumbling barefoot to the door. Cammie stopped then turned and blew me a kiss. "It would've been fun, Tom." I nodded as she closed the door behind her.

Her exit left me in silence and I felt the scalded indignity under the aching neon lights glowing like a jester's smile through the cracked shades of the window. I knew Cammie would drift back to her captivating crowd of late night hair-dyed disciples. The gutted nights would offer her another chance to right the wrongs of her shallow and calloused life, and Tom Judah would be forgotten over drinks and wounded, tic-tac smiles.

PART Three: On the Road

Odyssey Among Ruin

"You have made known to me the path of life." Psalm 16:11.

I did not sleep in the bed and fell asleep on the bathroom floor, awaking under mold scalloped curtains just before sunrise with my shoulder cramping from the yoked arm. I knew it was almost daylight by the smell. It was different. If you spend enough time in a combat zone, you pick up on these things and you know without knowing. The air was thicker and that thin sheen of moisture began to blanket the dim, gray, and clockless world; everything was quiet and we called this BMNT during our patrols in the unsecure red sectors of Iraq - **B**efore **M**orning **N**autical **T**wilight—just before sunrise when no one slept and the wars we fought were aroused from within that solitude.

I straightened my arm as a dog barked in the distance and I drifted back to a forgotten time spawned by the lowest tide of war…

"I saw at least two shooters in that second floor window!" Danko yelled across the street to Sergeant Johnson.

"Well Goddammit, can you take the cocksuckers out?" Johnson answered back.

"I dunno sergeant, every time Judah or I move the fuckers start shooting at us."

"Well it's gonna be a half hour before that engineer unit can clear the road to get a tank in here so you better think of something before one of those sand niggers gets a lucky shot in," Johnson yelled.

"Fuck me to tears," Danko swore and shoved a pinch of snuff into his lip then spat a brown stream. "You got any ideas, Judah? We sure as shit can't stay here forever and Johnson and the other guys can't cross the street and get to us."

"Way I see it, we're behind this wall and we can either wait it out and hope the tank gets lucky or we can try throwing a frag grenade through the window and get lucky that way," I said.

"Nope, too fucking far for a grenade."

"Fuck, I didn't think about that," I answered and took a pull from my water tube. "Where the hell is Frag anyway? That bastard can throw a grenade up a gnat's ass, but the fucker is never around when you need him."

"He's across the street with Johnson and the others."

I glanced across the road and saw Frag's grimy face hunkered into his shoulders. He looked my way and broke into a sucks to be you grin, then flipped me the bird.

I returned the gesture and mouthed the words, "God gave me a middle finger, too, motherfucker." He laughed and flipped me off again.

"The goddamn wall's too high to shoot over and we'll expose ourselves if we try to get a shot off from the side. What do you think, wait it out?" Danko asked.

"Shit no, I've got an idea." I looked at him and grinned. "We'll Alvin York their ass."

"We'll fucking what?" Danko laughed.

"Listen to me, you're taller than I am so I'll get on my knees and you stand on my back and get ready to shoot over the wall. When you're set, say the word and I'll start barking like a dog."

"Get the fuck out of here."

"No, listen to me. Once I start barking, sight in on the window and when one of those fuckers sticks his head out to see what we're doing, pop his ass," I explained and went to my knees.

Danko climbed on my back and peeked above the wall, "Alright, give 'em hell, Lassie."

I started barking and Danko started shooting. Three quick rounds and silence. "Well?" I asked.

"I think I drilled both of them," he said.

"You shot three times, are you sure?"

"Pretty fucking sure. Every time you barked, another head popped into view and I shot. I don't think there were three of them. I missed once and got him with the third shot when he crossed the room to the other side. Funniest goddamn thing I ever saw. Those camel fuckers must've thought we'd gone crazy with all that barking and shit," he laughed, stepping off my back and sitting down.

I rolled to my side, "My Dad was a Marine scout dog handler stationed in Pleiku and assigned a German Shepherd he named Alvin York. Hollywood made an old black and white movie about the real Alvin York after he won the Medal of Honor in World War One. He was just a ridge running moonshiner who grew up in the mountains of Tennessee and didn't want to fight in the war because of his religious beliefs."

"How in the hell did that win him the Medal of Honor?" he asked.

"Naw it ain't like that. He read some passage in the Bible and went and fought anyway. He was pinned down and started gobbling like a turkey so the krauts would stick their heads up. York was a dead-assed shot and every time he gobbled, he shot another kraut. The Germans finally surrendered to him so he single-handedly captured about a hundred krauts to win the medal."

"No shit?"

"No shit," I answered.

"Whatever happened to your Dad's German Shepherd?"

"I dunno, I can't remember or my Dad never said."

"I like a barking dog better than a gobbling turkey," Danko grinned and spat a stream of brown juice.

Johnson started calling Danko 'Dog' from that day until the morning he was killed.

I snapped back and remembered overhearing my Dad telling Uncle Frank about 'Nam' one night when I was supposed to be asleep. My Dad and his German Shepherd were both trained to kill but when their tour of duty was up and the government found out they couldn't deprogram the dog's killer instinct, he was euthanized. When the men came home, they had to deprogram alone. I guess that's why I never got that Christmas puppy, ever.

I folded my uniform and tucked it away inside my duffel bag, then checked out of the hotel. The bus station was closed for lunch and a plastic clock was arranged on the door with the hands positioned to show the time of the attendant's return. I sat outside on a faded bench and watched vacation-goers pass by while listening to their electric conversations.

The man sitting beside me was old and he wore a black Korean War veteran's ball cap and he could have been anybody. He lit a cigarette and his thumb was callused from a thousand other such strikes, his hair was cut short but not severe and his face betrayed no emotion, like he was a castaway from a dark civilization. You see men like these dressed conservatively or they might be wearing work clothes and they are equally at home walking out of an office building or into a department store. In fact, they each look exactly like an older version of you and you like a younger version of them. If these men were to walk by you later today, you wouldn't give them a second look. They don't stand out. They are just anonymous human beings walking by and the nature of that hidden fidelity so becomes them.

The trouble is they are not like other guys. They seem just a little too ordinary and yet they are anything but. You can tell by their eyes that they have endured hard years of combat and there are shared kinships born from that embrace.

"You must be either a Marine or Army Special Operations," he said to me and reclined back, interlocking his hands behind his head.

"I'm a Marine. What made you say that, sir?"

"Your haircut and the way you're watching everything and everyone."

"You were in Korea?" I asked changing, the subject from me to him.

"Yup."

"You see any combat?"

"Enough that I don't ever want to see it again."

"It still bothers you after all these years?" He looked at me and nodded slightly.

"The old man upstairs knew what he was doing when he gave mankind the passion for bloodshed and that in itself was God's cruelest joke of all. He placed violence in the bones of all men so its appetite would become insatiable once combat called it forth. I don't think I'll ever make peace with those horrible memories and my conscience will keep fighting that war every day for the rest of my life. You better remember that because Korea was fifty years ago for me. If you were in

Iraq, that means your battle is just getting started, son." I nodded as a woman across the street waved and yelled to him. The man stood and stretched and started towards her. "You take care of yourself and have a good time in Vegas," he said and patted my shoulder.

"Yes sir."

"Remember, what happens in Vegas stays in Vegas," he yelled back to me and then disappeared into the ordinary world of which he was as I let my living world fade with him…

I knew something was up when Sergeant Johnson told us to stand down as we had some "specials" coming into the compound to refuel and re-equip. We had never seen any of the Special Operations private security guys, and it was even more unusual given that they were ex-Army types and this was solely a Marine base.

They were special, alright. Two Humvee's that had been reduced to oddly fabricated wrecks approached from the northwest. The vehicles carried no markings, had armor-plates welded here and there, and bore plundered Soviet weapons on their turrets—the lead Hummer sported a Type 54, 12.7mm machinegun that was originally intended to be an anti-aircraft gun and the second vehicle had some strange kind of automatic grenade launcher mounted up top. The occupants were clearly American, but they had long hair, some had full beards, and all were wearing sunglasses and various non-military headgear.

It was *Bozo* who noticed the heads first. Attached to the lead *Humvee's* grill were two decapitated and obviously *Arabic* human heads hanging by a rappelling cord—the scraped heads bobbled and spun as the vehicle navigated the dunes around our camp. Hypnotic eyes and lips pouting in that feral curl of a *Jihad's* death.

"*Jesus H. Fucking Christ,*" Johnson grunted as he trotted to the lead vehicle.

Bozo and I approached so we could get a better look at these alien creatures while Johnson conversed with the team leader. They all carried *Soviet* small arms as pillaged souvenirs and were dressed in a ragtag way—the only thing military about them were their pants. One of the men wore a t-shirt emblazoned with the words "What happens in *Vegas* stays in *Vegas.*" The word *Vegas* was scratched out and the word *Iraq* was scrawled above it. The man jumped from the lead *Humvee* and lit a cigarette, then stuck it into one of the heads' mouth, drawing a few chuckles from the rest of the group. It gave me chills, but at the same time, I was glad that these guys were on our side. They understood the horror of war and yet they didn't seem burdened by its necessities.

The team leader was about 6'4" and wore a *Chicago White Sox* baseball hat and sported *Oakley* sunglasses. Johnson addressed him stiffly, "What in the hell do you think this is, some kind of a goddamn carnival? Those fucking heads are gonna draw a lot of the wrong attention if anyone gets sight of this and that shit is gonna stick to my platoon."

Mr. White Sox tipped his Oakley's down, revealing deadpan and delicious eyes. He smiled like some vendor of war selling past depravities and soothed Sergeant Johnson in a calm voice, "Now come on, sarge, these were righteous kills—they drew down on us with RPGs and we dispatched 'em. Besides, weren't you in Fallujah? Didn't you see what the fucking Hajis did to some of your Marines? If they want to cut off American heads, we'll cut their fucking heads off as paybacks—an eye for an eye, sarge." He drew his thumb across his throat and grinned. "It ain't anything personal to these motherfuckers... So if it ain't personal to them it will be to us and that's the way we're gonna roll."

"All I'm saying is that you never know who may be watching—we had Fox News out here a week or so ago," Johnson answered in a more obliging tone.

A few of the Mr. White Sox's men chuckled at the mention of the media and their team leader continued, again with a smile, "My dear, concerned Marine Sergeant. As a matter of fact, the day before we ended their hostilities, these same heads were chatting it up to CNN. And in case you haven't been told, we don't exist and we were never here. That is the official word from the powers that be and I would definitely appreciate it if you advised your men the same."

As they mounted up and drove off into the center of the compound to gas up and grab a bite of chow, Bozo and I stood staring at these strange warriors. Johnson did as well and wore a look that betrayed his true feelings—he admired these men and didn't give a flying fuck about the heads because he knew they were professionals. His protest had *been nothing more than a show lest one of us try to emulate the head trick after our next enemy encounter. Of course we never would because we still had to operate within a clearly defined set of rules.*

Two hours had passed unnoticed because I had forgotten to yoke my arm. I walked back inside the Greyhound terminal where a man behind a glass counter was reading a magazine. "Can I help you?" he asked, marking the page with a bent crease.

"I'd like to buy a ticket."

"To where?"

"I'm headed east towards Virginia, so anything that will get me closer will do."

"The last bus headed east pulled out at 10am," he answered, pointing at the departure board over his shoulder.

"Nothing else leaves today?" I asked.

"Everything that leaves after 10am is headed west to return the tourists home and pick up another batch and bring them here. Passengers quit taking the afternoon bus across the desert because of the heat, so Greyhound shut that route down. Most of the hotels are cheap, so if you want to stay the night, you can catch the 8am bus to Salt Lake City tomorrow morning. After that, you can buy another ticket that will get you further east from there."

"I've already spent one night in Vegas, sir."

"You didn't like it or it didn't like you?"

"A little of both, I guess."

"Remember, what happens in Vegas—"

"Stays in Vegas," I cut him off. "I've heard that a dozen times today."

"It's from the new commercial they're running on TV; kinda catchy don't you think?"

"Yes, sir. Is there an Internet café close by? I need to send my father an e-mail to let him know I'll be a few days late getting back home."

"Two blocks down the road on the left there's a Turkish coffee house with an internet connection." I thanked him and started to leave. "You still want that ticket?"

"Maybe tomorrow."

The café smelled of some faint and foreign incense, like the musty odor to disguise a hippie-head shop. A middle-aged man who reeked of curry and roasted goat welcomed me with "*assalamu alaikum.*" His beard was brutish in its wired weave of day-soaked stains that hid any smile he may have given. Peace be with you, he had said. I didn't like him. It came rushing back every time I walked into a store one of *their kind* owned, that war forced prejudice over their niggard smiles and false-friend attitudes. I had learned to hate the Muslim culture, their dress, and especially that mildewed stench of mistrust that clung about them in cloudless caution.

I hated them over there worse. Always the thumbs up smiles: "*America good,*" they'd chant as they ran alongside our Hummers with their grubby beggar hands held out. Those smiles widened when one of our vehicles blew up. *"Allah Akbar,"* they'd shriek when another American soldier ended up in a body bag. And we couldn't do a fucking thing about it. We were supposed to be the good guys fighting the good fight. Sergeant Johnson had a favorite ditty he'd taunt the crowds with:

"Sticks and stones may break my bones, but grenades and air strikes will silence Allah's throne."

Peace be with you? What the fuck did that part of the world know about peace? They had been in constant struggle trying to prove whose god was greater since the dawn of religion. I didn't try to change that view for them. Instead, I helped a few personally meet their version of god. I liked it then. In fact, I loved it. It haunted me now. I opened my laptop and punched out a quick letter to my father:

Dear Dad,

I miss you, I guess, and I don't mean that the way it sounds. I don't know what I miss on most days because I still don't feel much of anything. The war left me numb, almost barren on the inside. I guess I miss myself or what I was before I went to Iraq. It's like I'm searching for a memory that doesn't exist anymore. Maybe it never did. I don't know. That's why I quit taking the pills and going to therapy. Both of them left me in a world without answers. At least pain is something you can feel and anything is better than nothing.

We should have talked before I left. I know that now. There's so much I wanted to say to you and Mom when I came home from that war the first time.

I miss her and I don't want you to be lonely. I know you are, but I also know you'd never admit that to me, much less any one else.

You were right about me leaving and coming here, cooling off and getting this war out of my system, but you were always right about a lot of things. When I was over there, I missed home—Waynesboro, more than anything. It's weird, but that part of me is gone and I don't know why. I came back and everything was the same, but to me, everything was different, changed: you, Mom, my friends, and even Carrie. I guess she's remarried by now. Good for her. She deserved better than she got. She deserved better than me. I think chivalry was just another part of me that died over there in the sand.

I may be out of touch for a while, but don't worry Dad. I'm fine and on my way home. Miss you. I mean that the way it sounds.

Semper Fidelis,

Tom

It took two cups of a Turkish coffee the owner called *kahve* and a nasty pastry with the texture and taste of salty cardboard to finish and send the e-mail. I sat there staring at the owner's brutish beard, craving a can of beans and franks. I never liked beans and franks until I arrived in Iraq where everyone got them in care packages from home. We called them 'Hummer Nuggets' because you could heat a can on the manifold of the Humvee's engine for a few minutes, cover them in hot sauce, and then wolf them down with crackers if you got tired of eating the other rations. Odd that I remembered that now… I was forgetting significant parts of my life that had happened before the war, but remembering other unrelated tangents of the past in videographic clarity. It was happening all the time now. I looked down at my screensaver, a picture of me standing with a platoon of young, bare-chested men pointing towards various body parts sporting our unit tattoo—a bulldog with a set of devilish horns sprouting up between his ears, and under the animal was inscribed: *"The Prophets of Ruin."* It was the picture all ex-servicemen have stashed away somewhere: buddies standing around with weapons poised on hips, cigarettes dangling from wind-burned lips, and those badass grins covering the fear each man hid behind distant eyes. I snapped the lid closed and headed for the door.

"*Görüşmek üzere,*" Curry smell said without looking up. Then, not sure if I understood, he translated, "See you later."

Fuck you, I said to myself and left the place thinking about Sergeant Johnson's cold views on Turkey being a loose ally in the war.

"Unless they have single syllable names without a fucking hyphen, they're bad guys. The good guys have names like Ed, Frank, or Pete. The good guys speak English and like baseball and prom queens

sucking their dick in the back seat of Chevrolets, so if those cocksuckers answer to anything else, kill'em."

That was Sergeant Johnson and his devil dog way. I wondered what we would become once all the bad guys were dead. Good guys? I wasn't sure anymore, but one thing I did know: everybody who went to the sandbox came home a killer.

I wandered among a scatter of pawnshops decorating the seedy strip malls where stickers and local graffiti adorned the rust-stained concrete walls, a surfboard stuck in the sand beside a shop door brought back a jaundiced voice of my past: *"You can't surf with one fucking arm."*

One of the city's downtrodden residents wandered over to where I stood staring. "You got a cigarette I can bum, my man?"

"I don't smoke, sorry," I answered and nodded down the street. "Is there an Army surplus store around here?"

"A what?"

"A store that sells old military items and camping gear."

"Yeah, right down the road about a mile, you take a left on Commerce Street and there's a place like that on the right with a green tent displayed out front," he replied and eyed me up and down. "You a soldier or something?"

"I was, but not anymore. Thanks for the directions," I answered and started off.

"Gimme a dollar," he said. I stopped and turned.

"What?"

"Just gimme a dollar, man."

"Why?"

"For the directions I gave you," he answered and flashed a mouthful of grist-yellow teeth.

"Isn't it enough?" I asked.

"Enough of what?"

"Enough to be a decent human being without expecting some kind of fucking reward," I told him as my temper began to push me towards the edge.

"You gonna gimme a dollar or not, man?"

"No."

"Fuck you then," he said and walked away to reclaim his fragile day-to-day existence.

"Fuck you back," I answered.

The owner of Ranger Rick's Surplus had one of those purple birthmarks covering one side of his face. A Port Wine Stain they were called. I shook my head and looked at the odd and scarred facial stain as the man walked over to where I stood. "Can I help you with something?" he asked.

"I have a few items in my duffel bag and the bag itself I'd like to trade for a rucksack and a couple of canteens… maybe a few other things if we can work out some kind of deal."

"Alright, let's see what you have and then we'll talk business." I nodded and opened the flap and handed him my dress blue Marine uniform. "Son, this is something you earned and something you might want to hand down to your boy one day. I'm willing to work with you on the ruck, but I'd rather not take your dress uniform and medals."

"I don't think I'll be wearing it again and I can't see me having a son… not ever."

"What's your name?" he asked and rubbed the birthmark as if he might erase it from his face.

"Tom Judah."

"Tom, I'm Bud Larson, owner and operator of Ranger Rick's Surplus. Where are you from?"

"Virginia. Nice to meet you, Mr. Larson."

"Just getting free of Uncle Sam's grip are you?"

"Yes. sir," I said and emptied the duffel bag on the floor. "I have a few other odds and ends I need to get rid of to lighten my load."

"Alright, but why do you want a rucksack if you don't mind me asking?"

"I missed the last bus headed east by three hours, so instead of spending another night in Vegas, I decided I'd hitchhike to Salt Lake City."

"Jesus, son. That's over four hundred miles and most of that goes straight across the desert on I-15. What if no one stops to pick you up, did you think about that?"

"Yes, sir. That's why I wanted the canteens and I've got first hand experience when it comes to living in the desert," I answered. He nodded and grinned.

You boys are doing a good job over there and every damn one of us back here are prouder than hell of you guys. I'll tell you what, you keep the uniform and I'll drive you to Salt Lake City tomorrow morning. The reason all the buses heading east leave early is because of the heat, they can make the trip across the desert and back before it gets too hot."

"Thank you, but I think I'd rather walk."

"Are you sure? I don't mind at all, it's the least I could do for a returning vet."

"Thanks, Mr. Larson… but I could use the extra time to sort a few things out and get myself back on track."

"My son is in college so we have a spare room at the moment and you're welcome to spend the night," he offered. "I named him Chuck after Chuck Yeager. I was Air Force myself and met ole Yeager once. That man had balls the size of grapefruits to do some of the shit he did."

"I appreciate the offer but I think I'll hit the road while there's still enough daylight left."

"Alright, but you keep the uniform," he said. I shook my head.

"Just keep it here in case I ever want it back, Mr. Larson."

"I can do better than that. I'll vacuum seal it and when you get home, just look up the Ranger Rick's web page and drop me an e-mail. I'll send it out to you free of charge," he said, pulling a steel frame from a shelf. "You'll need the ruck's frame and a heavy Alice pack and at least three two-quart canteens."

I followed him around the store while he pulled various items from the dusty shelves: foot powder, water proof bag, green chem-lies, a K-bar knife, and enough military rations to last me a week. I went into the back room and changed into a set of tan UDT trunks and boots while Mr. Larson stayed out front adding other essentials to the side pouches of the ruck. I sandwiched my laptop inside an old sleeping bag and cinched the top straps down and shouldered the pack while he looked at the jagged scars on my leg.

"Shrapnel?" he asked, nodding at the pockmarks.

"Yeah, an IED took out the Hummer I was riding in."

He looked at the jagged lines and purple welts like they were a wake of sorrow and rubbed a hand over his birthmark. "I guess we all got to wear our scars before the world sometimes," he said.

"Yes, sir, my mother said that my scars were the maps of injustice."

"I guess she was right about that and I sure wish you'd change your mind and stay the night. My wife Sheryl Ann would love to have you and it'd be a nice change with Chuck being gone."

"Thank you, Mr. Larson. But you have done enough," I said. His gesture of gratitude was like so many others and it almost made everything worthwhile. Almost, but never quite enough.

"I thought you'd say that, so I called you a cab to drive you to the edge of town. A lot more could happen to you just trying to get out of the city than walking across the desert," he said as a car stopped and honked.

Bud yelled the directions from his shop door while I got in and before I could roll down the window to say good-bye, the cab jerked away from the curb and melted into the flow of traffic. I left Bud Larson rooted to where he stood, still wearing that birthmark before the world as if it were scalped flesh left to rot under an ancient and heatless sun. There are some scars we share willingly and others become a silent crucifix we resurrect to worship alone.

"Gonna take thirty minutes to get you to Interstate 15 and from there it's a straight shot to Salt Lake City," the driver said. I looked back, but Bud's door had closed behind him. I closed my eyes and let my head thump against the window like a rock, the hollow echo like that of a can being kicked to a sinister cadence along some blank and nameless road. I yawned and faded back to a hard time that was ruled by harder men...

We had stopped our patrol to take a break and wolf down our Meal Ready to Eat we had drawn as chow. I had chili mac, but Danko wanted to eat first, so I pulled watch. Fifty percent security during breaks. One man ate while his buddy stayed alert and covered him, and

Johnson stayed on our ass about this because you were most likely to start droning when you pulled security.

"I ain't real thrilled about another fucking MRE paradise lunch, Judah. All I want is the chocolate bar and a pinch of snuff, then you can eat."

"Fair enough," I yawned, resting a cheek on the butt of my rifle.

"Fucking Johnson can be a real prick sometimes," he said, chewing. "That cocksucker volunteered us for this patrol. Wasn't our goddamn turn." He unstrapped his k-pot, took it off, and sat on it.

"You better not let Johnson see your ass with that fucking k-pot off. You'll get volunteered for a bunch of other shit when we get back to the compound," I said.

"Fuck him," Danko grinned and extended his hand. "Let me steal a pinch of snuff off you."

"You out or just too cheap to buy your own snuff, you mooching cocksucker."

"Just give me a fucking pinch," he said, leaning over.

The large, jagged rock whistled down and caught Danko in the back of the head, ripping off the scalp and four inches of skull with it. He died like that. A grinning Prophet of Ruin mooching a pinch of snuff.

"Sergeant Johnson!" I screamed as my eyes panned to where I thought the stone thrower was perched above us.

Johnson came running up the sidewalk yelling, "What the fuck happened? Did anyone hear a shot?" he asked, passing by each of our positions. Our crazy-eyed lieutenant, the man Johnson had dubbed Wild Bill, met him at out location.

"It was a fucking rock," I told them.

"A fucking what?" Johnson barked, kneeling to check Danko.

"A big goddamn rock," I said again.

"I saw them from the rooftop above Danko and Judah. Two kids threw a big fucking brick or something, and then the little bastards took off across the top of the buildings and jumped into that alley," Wild Bill said, pointing skyward like he'd seen some heavenly light.

Motherfucker," Johnson swore and through gritted teeth seethed, "I'll take first squad and run those fuckers down, sir."

Wild Bill shook his head. "Negative that, we've only got thirteen men on patrol today and those alleys are owned by the Hajis. They'd cut you to ribbons from the rooftops."

Johnson cussed again, then yelled across the street to where the rest of the platoon pulled security. "Start watching the goddamn rooftops and if anyone sees anything move up there, including kids, waste their fucking ass. Waste their ass most fucking rikki-tick."

"All this because of a couple kids," I whispered. Johnson heard me.

"Little tigers grow up to be mean fucking lions don't they?" he replied, lighting a cigarette.

"Tigers don't grow up to be lions."

"What?"

"Tigers grow up to be tigers, Sergeant. Lions are a different breed of cat," I explained.

"You fucking think Danko gives a shit about tigers and cats, Mr. Animal Planet?" Johnson asked, spewing twin jets of smoke from his nose. "These fucking sand nigger kids grow up to find Allah's blessed Jihad so you get this through your fucking skull while we wait for Doc to bag Danko. I don't give a good flying fuck in hell what age these demon fucks are, if they pick up a rock or a stick or anything and try to hurt me or one of my men, I'm gonna kill'em. You better start toughening the fuck up and see it my way as well, or you'll end up like Danko: killed by some fucking kid with sticks and stones." He looked at me and stubbed the cigarette out on his palm. "Now ain't that a nice motherfucking letter I gotta send home to Mother Danko. Dear Mrs. Danko, it is with great regret to inform you that your son was killed by a camel fucker throwing a Goddamn rock."

He dropped one of Danko's two dog tags, I snatched it up and shoved it in my shirt pocket. I don't know why. Johnson spun the chain with the remaining dog tag on his finger and walked off across the street kicking a can. "Goddammit men, how many times I gotta tell you devil dogs to keep your fucking k-pots on? From now on, everyone sticks to my rules, every last fucking one of you."

"Hey, you crazy motherfucker. Hey Goddammit, wake the fuck up!" the cabbie shouted and grabbed my shoulder. I recoiled and snapped the knife-edge of my left hand against his throat, stopping it just short of doing any real damage.

"Don't ever put your hands on me ever again. Do you understand?" I said through clenched teeth and brought my hand away from his neck.

"Yeah… yeah, man. Just chill the fuck out, you were just thrashing all over the goddamn seat and it scared the hell out of me. It was like you were possessed or some shit."

"I was having a bad dream so no harm no foul," I answered and started to pull out my wallet when he stopped me.

"Bud's already covered your cab fare so keep your money," he said and I offered him ten bucks as a tip, but the shook off the offer.

"Bud took care of the tip as well by getting me a job when I got paroled." I nodded and got out.

"Be sure and thank Mr. Larson for me the next time you're in his store," I said and shouldered the rucksack.

"I'll do that and you keep heading east down I-15 and you'll eventually wind up in Salt Lake City," he said, pointing through the windshield. I nodded and the man leaned forward and gave me a mock salute mouthing the words 'take care' as the car completed a u-turn and then disappeared back to the endless ribbon of road and then nothingness.

PART Four: Angels and Demons

Salt Lake City

"Public opinion is a weak tyrant compared with our own private opinion. What a man thinks of himself, that is what determines, or rather indicates his fate." Henry David Thoreau

Clouds began rising into columns of sinister thunderheads as the electric sky sent flues of lightning across the heavens like a Technicolor dream untainted by any creature. I stretched and readjusted my pack, then pushed further into the defacement beyond. It felt like I was on another patrol in a similar desert wasteland called back from parallel days not so distant. In Iraq, the length of our combat treks was always measured by just-around-the-next-curve-in-the-road increments. I picked up my pace and half-expected to hear Frag asking Sergeant Johnson, *"How much further?"* and Johnson would always answer, *"Just around the next curve in the road."* The curves kept coming and we kept marching.

I checked my watch and started counting the cars that passed by my thumb as a way to take my mind off the endless road. Houses grew scarce until the last few were rancid shacks with two glassless windows splitting an open and abandoned doorway. The final yard had a yipping mutt that was no more than a rib-showing mongrel rooted to a permanent leash of neglect. The creature looked at me with cautious eyes and growled, I wondered if the dog was only responding to some inner voice and that odd revelation brought the name Alvin York to mind. The person was familiar and yet I couldn't quite place him. Maybe we had served together in Iraq, I wasn't sure anymore. A rumble of thunder shook free those secluded thoughts and I looked skyward as a falling star smoked a trail against the darkened and bitter skyline. I watched as the burning gossamer tail finally extinguished to some distant place beyond the horizon.

I pulled free the K-Bar knife Bud Larson had shoved into the side pouch of my ruck and cut the dog loose, his eyes never left mine as if this were some showdown between humanity and his canine instincts. The animal watched me walk away and continued to trot in that rotund and paw-worn circle like his leashed world still existed, if it ever did at all.

The storm was bearing down and I needed to find shelter before the rain and earthly elements began their soaking choreography of ruin. I dropped off the road and walked a fence line until I found a concrete drain line running under the highway. The inside seemed like some carved and earthly bowel with the far end partially obstructed by barbed wire and rain-washed debris. A spear of lightning sent chevrons of light across the opening that illuminated odd scrawls of adolescent graffiti on the beveled walls. I ducked into the manmade cavern and broke open a green chem-lite as water attacked my rabbit-hole world in sheets of unrelenting vengeance, serrated jags of light flaring as if illumination was needed to guide this rain rendered war. I needed company in the way that the lonely savor a memory when locked in solitude.

The cracks of thunder increased in ear drumming repetition as spears of shifting radiance seemed to answer the mysteries of those concrete walls and their hieroglyphic runes. The wind blew through the enclosure with a hollow sound like blowing across an empty pop bottle.

I pulled out the iPod and plugged it into my ears, closing my eyes and letting the unknown tune drown out the storm's fury. I hadn't downloaded this song. *"What the hell?"* I thought at first and then shook it off. Maybe my ex-wife had downloaded some of her music before we divorced. The wind seemed to penetrate the sanctity of my grotto and time passed while the squall uncoupled my world, leaving the flat taste of scorched cotton in my mouth. I tried to spit the dry tang free, but nothing came out. I broke and shook another chem-lite to life when a greenish cataract of light seemed to relight the faces of those war dead ghosts of my combat days past.

The faces and voices began calling out as I fought sleep behind my yoked-arm world, calling out as though they offered to take my foreign hand and guide me away to their land of past sorrows. All traces of color vanished to gray and black, and the scribbled walls of the tunnel, slick with congealed moisture, began closing in.

Lightning burnt through the drain's opening in an explosion of intensity and the faces stared at me like obscene visitants unleashed on this the world of half-lived men.

I stripped out of my clothes and dropped to my knees, chanting in poached Pentecostal tongues as the rain stung my back like an earthly penitence. Sergeant Johnson's voice broke through my guarded wall of jaded memories.

"Judah, these people are nothing more than a bunch of fucking animals, little brown sandal wearing demons. They sent us here to be the demonslayers and that's what we're gonna do. You gotta become a mean motherfucker in their sandy shithole world, so toughen the fuck up. Never show weakness and always make them fear you because their fear of you is your power over them. Commit and execute, that's the devil dog way."

"Doesn't that bother you?" I asked.

Johnson lit a cigarette, "Doesn't what bother me?"

"All of the blood we're spilling, Sergeant?"

"Not one fucking bit. This is my job and I love doing it."

"Isn't that compromising your faith in God?"

"Try letting your faith stop a bullet," Johnson answered and took another drag off his cigarette.

"There are no atheists in foxholes, Sergeant."

"Yeah, well," he said and grinned, "I ain't found God waiting for me in a foxhole either."

"That's a black and white way of looking at life and death, Sergeant Johnson."

"Over here, I am a God of both."

I blinked awake, naked and cold, shivering inside goose-pimpled reptilian flesh that I wore like a leper's scars, both unfeeling and unclean. Water dropped in soft patters to the desert sand while roots drank the fluid before the sun could banish the moisture with the rising heat. The gray clouds moved across the blue divide toward a more worthy prey, trailing dirty thunder and blood red skies in their wake.

I crawled through the storm-ravaged foliage, searching for my clothes and scanning the surroundings for my belongings. I found my shirt and pants flattened against the sand as if some distant tide had left them there. The earth smelled musty and damp like a predator's lair in some godless realm of deception with retribution still unpaid. I grabbed my pack and realized there was nothing here and no place to hide from my past miseries and sorrows. It's too bad that sleep was necessary as it had now evolved into a fast forward button to relive yesterday's agony. Suffering had now become my greatest teacher on earth.

I dressed and hobbled up the embankment to the interstate like some reeking effigy sent to greet each motorist as they sped past me and my wretched day. Regret is the hardest currency in life when repentance has no known value. The wind tossed cirrus clouds along the skyline like feathers from alien birds descending upon a pale and crumbling globe. I stumbled by the tire-flattened carcass of some unidentified animal and the broken highway seemed to wear that husk as if it were an unfeeling scab. *"You got off easy,"* I said to the lifeless creature and continued my trek deeper into a new day with a less-than-bright future. A bleached and weathered billboard planted on the side of the road advertised an ultimatum to all travelers, *'Last chance for gas 1 mile ahead.'*

The small station shimmered on the heat-waved expanse like an oasis sprung up from the desert ground. A man wrapped in filthy overalls leaned against the doorjamb as I walked across the gravel lot. "Your car break down or something?" he asked, eating a sandwich, his grease-stained fingers left dark prints on the white bread as he tore off chunks with his teeth and washed them down with a carton of milk.

"No sir, I walked."

"Walked, from where?"

"Vegas," I said, dropping my ruck on the planked floors.

"What in the hell did you do that for?" he asked, chewing the last bite.

"I missed my bus and thought it was a good idea at the time, but I didn't count on that thunderstorm last night."

"That was a damn good'n wasn't it?" he grinned and tossed the empty carton over his shoulder onto a growing pile of liter beyond the door. "Most of the thunder boomers in this part of the state last about ten minutes, but that'n shook this ole station all night long, almost seemed like it was possessed by demons or something."

"Yes, sir, I thought the same thing," I answered with a shiver.

"Did the rain catch you out in the open?"

"I got lucky and found an old drain line running under the road a few miles back and spent the night in there."

"Where you headed?" he asked, dusting the crumbs from his coveralls as if it mattered.

"Salt Lake City," I said, looking over his shoulder. "I'd buy a drink off you if you've got one to spare.

"What kind you want?"

"Anything that's cold will do." He nodded and motioned me inside with his head.

"Lemme see what I've got," he said, opening an old icebox. "How bout a Coke?"

"A Coke would be fine right about now. I need the extra sugar anyway."

He sat the can on a dog-eared counter and leaned his elbows against the tabletop like a card dealer. "There's an ole boy that runs a big rig through here bout lunch time every day with a daily load going to Salt Lake City, he's a good ole shit and I could probably get him to give you a ride if you want it."

"I'd really appreciate that, sir," I said and offered my hand. "I'm Tom Judah, thank you for the Coke."

He shook my hand and declined any payment. "I'm Junior Baker and you don't owe me a thing for the drink."

"You sure?"

"Yup, it's the least I could do for any man crazy enough to walk from Vegas to here," he said, looking at my OD green rucksack. "You must've been a soldier."

"I was a Marine," I said, finishing the drink. "Is there a bathroom I can use to wash up, Mr. Baker?"

"Round back," he replied, handing me a key that was attached to an old car engine's piston. I hefted the contraption, looking at the rusty dome. "I put that on there so people would remember to bring the key back," he explained with a grin.

I cleaned up and repacked my laptop in the backpack, I was tired and it was taking a toll on me. Focusing on anything for more than a few minutes took considerable effort. I shouldered my rucksack and looked into the mirror at the rebuked reflection unhorsed by the long and fraudulent nights. Beyond the odd-colored and misgiving eyes, I saw that dim sinister burn that all combat vets have and hide so well. I stood there staring at my reflection and the devil dog tattoo on my shoulder longer than I realized, thinking back to the Marine Corps boot camp I had endured on Parris Island. It was the drill sergeant's job to create that budding seed of the killers they trained by putting us through a daily routine of push-ups and before-daylight runs to strengthen the hearts that pounded out that killer blood.

"You alright?" the grimy owner asked, knocking on the door. "You've been in there for over an hour."

"Yes sir, just finishing up, Mr. Baker."

"Alright, I got you that lift I told you about so as soon as I get his rig filled with diesel, he'll be pulling out. I wouldn't want you to miss another ride," he laughed. It was another gracious gesture in my favor that never quite seemed to balance these scales of my misfortune.

The truck was belching smoke from its twin stacks like fangs from a beast, and Mr. Baker was talking to the driver when I walked up. "I was thinking about something you told me earlier," he said, and held my rucksack while I climbed into the cab.

"What was that?" I asked, taking the ruck and shutting the door.

"Son, I've owned this station for damn nigh forty years, been up and down this ole highway so many times I could walk it with my eyes closed, and there ain't no drain line running under the road anywhere," he said.

The man driving the tractor trailer was morbidly obese from too many greasy meals at rest stops and all-nighters. The road is a weary and lonesome place, he explained, tapping his large gut as if the gesture would alleviate any further explanation about his size. He kept looking from the road to me and it was making me nervous, cautious, and vigilant as the white lines on the interstate wound away like ticker tape.

"One of your eyes is brown and the other one looks like it was split down the middle with half of it being brown and the other side blue," the man said, squinting.

"It's a rare form of heterochromia."

"Heterochromia?"

"It's a gene my father's side of the family carries and it usually hits every third or fourth generation when someone is born with different colored eyes," I answered.

"So heterochromia means different colored eyes?"

"Yes."

"Does your father have eyes like yours?"

"No, actually the gene skipped about three generations before it got to me. My great grandfather was the first one we knew about that had different colored eyes. He was born with one brown eye and one blue eye. My family said he was a strangely devout man and once his children were gone, he left his home and vanished into the mountains of Virginia with nothing but his long rifle and a Bible. The Cherokee called him *The man who fights with Himself*" and he lived like a recluse in those hills for years."

"What was his real name?"

"Reuben Judah."

"He sounds like he'd have a story or two to tell if he were still alive."

"Yes, sir, he's become a bit of a legend around home."

"Why's that?" he asked.

"The old people used to tell us kids that he was still wandering those mountains, preaching among the wilds and fighting the devil and his inner demons. I guess you could say he was our redneck version of the boogeyman. I suppose it was their old fashioned way of getting us kids to behave in church by scaring us with stories about him."

"You mean he went crazy over religion?"

"I dunno, maybe I guess. I think I remember being told that something bad might have happened to him during the Civil War," I shrugged.

"So no one knows whatever happened to him?"

"No, they don't have any record of when or if he died."

"What do you mean, if he died," the driver asked with a jowly shit-eating grin.

"I mean that every year, some hunter will report seeing a man dressed in buckskins wandering the woods and preaching to the mountains of his earthly sins. That's how the story of Reuben Judah was told to me, that he was a pious and violent man who disappeared among those high ridges to atone for his wrongdoings. Are you asking me if I believe that?" He looked at me, waiting for an answer as if some grand hoax were about to be revealed. "If you are, then my answer is no, I don't think he's alive or the boogeyman because I don't believe in ghosts," I explained and shivered.

"You alright?" he asked.

"Yes, sir, just tired from walking all day yesterday," I lied and yawned. "How much further to Salt Lake City?"

"A couple three hours if the traffic cooperates," he answered and blew the big rig's air horn at a passing convertible being driven by a woman. "Gotta love the seat covers you see passing by."

"Yes, sir. I'd like to grab a quick nap if it's alright." He nodded and reached behind his seat and offered me a small pillow. "Wake me up when we get to Salt Lake City and I'll buy you dinner before I head to the bus station."

"That's a deal," he said. "I'll do you one better than that: there's a truck stop across from the Greyhound terminal and we'll stop there." I nodded and plugged my ears into my iPod and yoked an arm behind my back to avoid any further conversation about my misguided family history. I realized then that the previous night's struggle I endured had brought my sanity down another notch… and there was nothing I could do to correct it.

The truck stop was a flood of callused men and other lonely road gypsies all haggling over what route to take or where to stop for the best food as my plump companion swung his rig among that chaos of trucks, trailers, and semi-crustaceous humanity.

"You ever have a nickname?" my driver asked, sawing the wheel. I rubbed my eyes as the rig came to a stop and the air brake hissed with a pop. I recoiled and ducked my head at the sudden sound.

"No, sir," I lied and blushed.

"My given name is Carl Bishop, but my handle on the road is Pig Pen. It's sort of a nickname we use on our CB radios."

I nodded and looked across the street at the bus station, "I'll slip across the road and get my ticket if you want to go inside and grab us a table."

"You want me to order something for you?" he asked.

"That'd be fine and go ahead and get what you want and have the waitress put everything on one ticket," I said, jumping from the sideboard to the ground.

"I got a big appetite," he grinned.

"Yes, sir, and I have a big wallet." He laughed and chocked the truck's tires.

I went across the street towards the Greyhound terminal while my large driver waddled over and chatted with fellow truckers about the hazards of their road itinerant ways. The bus depot smelled of stale urine and exhaust fumes, and the floors and benches were littered with both the derelicts and delights of a frail and forgotten humanity. I purchased a ticket to Denver leaving at 8pm, allowing me two hours to eat and ready myself for a new chapter and just another day in paradise. On the sidewalk, I waited for a break in traffic to cross back over to the truck stop while two dark-skinned boys with their hats turned backwards began rapping. Hip-hop had now crossed all boundaries and conquered even the redneck trucker world, it seemed. The rhyming beat of their lyrics and cadenced voices had me zoning out again, it was becoming unsafe and happening to me more and more…

Johnson was running us around the compound on one of our few days off. Mentally tough and physically strong went hand in hand with Sergeant Johnson. Our feet struck the ground to the cadence calling that kept his devil dogs in step to his voice:

"We follow our leader, our demonslaying God,

We're the prophets of ruin in his demonslaying squad.

They sent us to fight in this foreign land,

Devil Dogs killing in the Iraqi sand.

If I die in the combat zone,

Just box me up and ship me home.

Flag on my coffin, medals on my chest,

Blood on the hands that did their best."

"Hey, dipshit, a fucking car is gonna whack your ass if you don't get out of the road," a voice spoke like it came from a tunnel. One of the young rappers leaned over to grab my shoulder and pull me back onto the sidewalk when I stopped him.

"I'm alright, just wasn't paying attention," I said, avoiding his touch and trotting back across the highway.

Carl Bishop and his immense girth occupied the entire side of a booth and he waved me over when I walked into the restaurant. "I just sat down and haven't had a chance to order anything yet. Did you get your ticket?" he asked.

"Yeah, I pull out around eight," I said, sitting down and opening a menu.

The waitress came to our booth and took our order while I looked down at her shoes—white nurses shoes. It reminded me of my mother dying and the nurses coming in and out of her room, clearing the beeping alarms that always seemed to be going off until they shut the tubes and monitors down for good. I looked down at their shoes, fighting back the tears, ashamed that they would see me cry, ashamed at showing any form of weakness. Never show weakness—that's the devil dog way.

"So how far are you going?" Carl asked, putting his menu back in its holder.

"Virginia. How about you?"

"I'll complete my run and head back to Vegas after I get eight hours of rest because of the new DOT laws," he smirked and rubbed his pudgy face. A young woman walked by our section carrying a suitcase and sat at the booth opposite us. Carl grinned and winked at me as the waitress returned and placed two glasses of ice water and silverware on our table. "What do you think," he asked.

"About what?" Carl answered me with a nod of his head towards the girl. "Oh, she's pretty," I answered as three men walked over to where she sat.

"You need a ride?" one of the men asked, noticing the suitcase and sat down beside her.

"No thank you, and I would appreciate it if you would find somewhere else to sit. I didn't ask for your company," she replied without looking up from her menu.

"You don't need to be a fucking bitch about it," one of his friends laughed and that callus use of language pissed me off.

"You men need to watch your mouths," I said. The talker looked me over while the other two grouped up, and then all three walked over to where Carl and I sat.

"Oh shit," the pudgy driver muttered.

"You say something," the loud mouth talker said, sizing me up while the two guys by his side snickered. They were toadies, followers, and backers. Not talkers. The people around our booth made that noise, like a blowing a whistle in reverse, they sucked air back through their lips with an audible *'you gonna take that shit'* hiss of contempt as I fought to control my rising temper.

One of the toadies leaned over and whispered to the one who'd insulted the woman. "Fuck it. Let's just go, Pete."

"If you wadgobbling pieces of shit have something to say, say it out loud," I said, not liking their whispering, and started to get out of my seat when a hand grabbed my shoulder.

I followed the arm to a smooth face sporting a thin Snidely Whiplash mustache. He smiled showing capped teeth and soothed in an almost feminine voice. "Just chill the fuck out, friend."

The bluntness of his statement uncoiled that passion. I felt its touch and relished in that wave of pre-battle excitement. It was the only feeling other than pain that I could identify. I was sliding down slowly to that place where violence of action rumbles and begins its inevitable eruption.

"Buddy, you got about three fucking seconds to get your greasy dickskinner off my shoulder or I'll break it the fuck off." He didn't move, so I leancd in closer and asked, "You got shit in your ears, cocksucker? If I gotta tell you again to get that pickle grabbing shitpicker off my shoulder, I'll kick your fucking ass so high, you'll have to take your shirt off when you squat to take a shit."

The sleeves of his expensive polo shirt were rolled up, showing a set of smooth tanning bed arms. He obliviously came from money and the people of wealth around my hometown were the first to build fences and walls around their homes to further isolate themselves. They eventually lost touch with the harder edge of life and lived a sheltered and honed existence in their half-finished civilization of glass towers.

Snidely put more pressure on my shoulder like the dried grip of an ugly nun with her bony fingers bearing down. "Was I talking to you in the first place?" he asked. The tension at our table reeked with an issue yet settled and the air between us seemed to question the topic. Snidely thought I was bluffing. I never bluffed.

I stood up, facing all three men, and shrugged off his thin hand as if it were an affliction. The hand seemed to hover in the air and Snidely started to say something, but he hesitated. That's where the untrained fail. They hesitate and you never hesitate, that's not the way of the goat. His indecision was the extra pressure that flicked *that* switch and the inevitable happened in a flash.

I grabbed his hand, taking a step back to pull him off balance, then lunged forward, driving my fist straight at his hyoid bone. I fully intended to kill him: crush his hyoid bone to collapse the trachea and he'd be unconscious in seconds, dead in minutes. I missed the fatal area, but still caught him in the throat. You know when you've caught someone good, there's a certain bone and gristle feel to the crunching blow. Solid. Snidely collapsed with white eyes rolled back in his head and bloody snot bubbles popping from his nose in visceral snaps of full laryngospasm. The flagrant sound of those snaps and gasps revived a whispered memory and opened the door to all things of violence.

I heard yelling above the scrapes of chairs and shuffling footsteps. Like muffled sounds from a cave, they were as hollow and as nondescript as applause. I reacted out of habit. Secure the area and follow up on multiple targets of opportunity; eliminate the threat.

I heard a woman's voice yelling something unintelligible above the clamor as one of the men broke and ran towards the door, but his other snickering friend hesitated. I kicked him in the chest, meaning to break a rib and puncture a lung or major artery. The blow sent him hurtling backwards, knocking over two rows of tables as both food and people scattered across the floor. Children started screaming and crying.

I looked at the man as he crab-crawled away from me. "You wanted to be a badass so get up motherfucker."

Carl Bishop said something and I turned to find him kneeling beside the man I had just punched in the throat. That pissed me off. "Move out of the way, fat man, I'm not done with this sonofabitch," I said, walking towards him and I meant it. The rage had passed and I was now on full-auto and occupying a place of familiarity—violence and killing.

"He's had enough," Carl said, shielding the gasping, terrified man with his meaty arm. A hand touched my shoulder and I spun around, knocking the hand free with my fist cocked to deliver another punch.

"No," the suitcase woman said, stumbling back and crossing her arms to protect her face.

"Don't you fucking touch me like that again, ever," I said, lowering my fist.

"Fine," she snapped and left the place without another word.

I looked around the restaurant and those faces staring back at me wore that tight-lipped stare of disgust, like they had been gypped by some quarter-a-head sideshow freak. I stood there before them and matched each stare with one of my own like this was normal, like this was just another part of my boring day.

Snidely wobbled to his feet and gimped on unsteady legs to his friends standing at the door, still holding his throat and looking at me warily with silver dollar eyes. The trio chatted and pointed in my direction, then left the place with a renewed chance of living to see tomorrow.

PART Five: Highs and Lows

Two Doors

"Forgiving does not erase the bitter past. A healed memory is not a deleted memory. Instead, forgiving what we cannot forget creates a new way to remember. We change the memory of our past into a hope for our future." Lewis B. Smedes

Specks of blood stained my hands like the remnants from a strange fetish, so I wiped them on a napkin and stared at the tarnished relic as if it were a demented inkblot test, thinking that perhaps the answer to bloodshed itself was hidden there among those red pictograms. I shoved the stained paper inside my pocket, not understanding why I was collecting these aberrant tokens and then left the restaurant like a soiled and retreating infidel. Across the road, a man wearing a Greyhound uniform was walking from his car towards the bus terminal when I trotted over. "Is there a bathroom close by? The one inside the station is out of order."

"If you're a Greyhound passenger, you can use that temporary port-o-potty," he said pointing toward a turquoise booth.

"Yeah, I got a ticket for the 8pm bus to Denver."

"That's my bus and we'll start loading up in thirty minutes," he answered, looking at his watch then ducked through the doors as the girl who I'd almost punched stepped to the sidewalk with her suitcase. I avoided the woman's stare and went inside the portable stall, locking the door. I sat down, listening to the conversations coming from the sidewalk and I let the mess of my life pass by with them. I checked my watch, pulled the stained napkin out, looked at the crimson marks as if they were the emblems on some holy banner, and then stored it away inside my ruck. I unscrewed a canteen and poured water across my battle ravaged hands until they were clean. "*What the fuck is wrong with me,*" I thought and closed my eyes...

I stepped outside our billets and went to the port-o-john we used in place of a regular latrine, behind the cubicle, I overheard Sergeant Johnson talking to Captain Benson, the camp psychologist. We had dubbed Benson 'Dr. Feelgood' and he openly resented the unearned moniker, calling it both adolescent and childish. They were talking about one of the devil dogs in my platoon and it didn't take me long to realize it was me they were conversing about.

"Isn't that what we want, men who respect their superior officers and follow their orders without question?" Johnson asked.

"Yes, but there are guidelines we need to follow... even in war, Sergeant."

"What kind of fucking guidelines, sir?"

"I don't want to go into that in great detail, but Corporal Judah is beginning to lavish in the violence and he is starting to collect trophies

from any conflict he has been through and survived," Benson explained.

I could see Johnson grinning at the man through the metal vent, "What your profession might call trophies we Marines call the spoils of war."

"You can call them what you want, but that won't change the facts. Did you know that a recent study conducted by the FBI Behavioral Science Unit on serial killers found that many of those murderers kept mementos of their victims as a way of filling some void in their demented lives?"

"Well I appreciate that tidbit of information, sir. But Judah is staying right where he's at for now."

"I think you're making a bad decision and I wish you would reconsider my offer and try to work with me on this, Sergeant. I have counseled Corporal Judah several times and I've noticed that he has begun to use you and the military as a surrogate to replace his deceased mother."

Johnson shook his head and lit a cigarette, "I can't send him back to the states."

"Why? One man is easily replaced, Sergeant."

"Because he's one of my best soldiers and I actually wish I had an entire platoon of men just like him."

"You can't be serious, Sergeant Johnson."

"You're goddamn right I am, sir. I need men who will not hesitate when the time comes to kill. If a man hesitates in combat, he shifts the

advantage to the enemy and I face losing one of my men, and I'm not
here to bury American soldiers."

"What are you here for then?"

"To let these sand niggers bury their people instead of me burying
mine."

I pulled myself back from that crepuscular world as the rumble of a bus sounded and I stepped into the eternal night and watched as it belched away from the terminal. I took off running with my rucksack flopping against my back and caught up to the vehicle before it exited the parking lot. I was trotting along behind the front tire and banging on the bus's closed bat-wing entry when it stopped and the doors peeled back.

"I thought you had changed your mind," the driver grunted.

"No, sir," I said, handing him my ticket. "I fell asleep until I heard you pulling away."

"Good enough," he said, punching my stub and handing it back. "Go ahead and grab yourself a seat."

The young woman I had almost punched from the truck stop sat behind the driver with her suitcase between her legs like a proper Catholic girl at confession. She looked up as I walked by and I avoided her curious eyes as the rhombus craft lurched forward with a pneumatic hiss and took me deeper into the darkness of another destination I no longer controlled.

A Greyhound bus is an ever-changing kaleidoscopic vessel of miss-matched humanity, and I began a ten-hour ride of profanity and lice among the lesser fools of life's indecent offerings. They were the survivors without saviors and I fit right in their demonic journey where no apology would right the wrong of it. My arm stayed yoked behind my back like some single-limbed deviant fighting sleep with depravation as my guide on this forlorn highway of deception. I fought the constant cyanotic smell of curry-laced passengers, failed Hollywood hopefuls reinventing their lives after surviving the prostitution cesspool, socially demented elderly, and a host of nameless simpletons with no other recourse of travel.

The road ground away beneath the bus as I fought sleep among my company of undesirables. I kept a blanket covering my head and watched the scenery change in fleeting waves like a slideshow. The woman from the truck stop kept twisting around in her seat and I could sense her stare beyond my covered and protected world. The bus finally stopped in a crusty place outside a Navajo reservation near some unnamed town to refuel and exchange drivers before finishing the route to Denver. It was a rural and crabby place with small trinket shops selling odd handmade items to the sparse and declining tourist trade.

Old women sat in a gaggle before makeshift pottery wheels with their brown and gnomish feet tromping the wooden pedal as cupped hands cradled the spinning clay. Their squared fingers moved deftly up and down the muddy urns until the project slowly took form. The mimicked crockery was copied from the earliest forms of their ancestral artistry and all of the crones seemed lost in some primeval contemplation, perhaps briefly sharing the knowledge of their creation, but keeping the thought of inspiration muted and unvoiced.

An old Indian man watched me with deep set eyes, his face a carved effigy of war map wrinkles and totem pole smiles. A grey parrot clutched his thin shoulder with scaly feet and chatted away with its fowl tongue to all who passed by, offering worldly wisdom for a peanut reward that the day-tripping misers could purchase from the man for a nickel. The bird watched me with its beady eyes and waddling head and then went silent and looked down. The old man passed the creature a nutty treat and then stared up at me as I cycled back to another time.

My ex-wife had bought an African Parrot she named 'Pepper' to keep her company while I was away, and that bird knew the real deal. When I came home after my first tour of duty, the nightmares about the war began and I would awake in the wee hours of the morning fighting with my wife while she held me, telling me it was only a dream. I didn't want to be held then. Instead, I pushed her away and crawled into a drug-induced realm to fight my demons alone. The only time I heard the bird talk was after we fought and she would leave to stay at her mother's house. I sat there riding out my buzz listening to that bird say over and over, "*Redneck love, baby.*"

The old one was speaking to a teenage boy in a language I did not know and gestured with a crow-clawed hand in my direction.

"What did he say?" I asked, walking over.

"My grandfather says you are fighting a war you cannot win," the boy translated.

"The war is over for me, I'm not a soldier anymore," I replied and dropped a dollar in their beggars cup. The boy spoke to the old man and he shook his grizzled head.

"Grandfather says the war your fight is not of this world and asks if you want to make the journey to rid yourself of what lies beyond the doors," the boy said and the old man shook the hollow cup while looking skyward with chalky eyes of the sightless.

"He's blind?" I asked. The boy nodded and the old man continued to natter away in that guttural tongue of his ancestors.

"Grandfather says his eyes are blind to this world but they are open to the one beyond, the place you will need to see so you can win your battle. He says there is a spirit door that you have closed to this world and you must open that gateway to journey back into your past."

"I already know what I'm fighting. Thanks, but no thanks."

"He also said that you know your demons but they know you as well."

"How much?" I asked. The boy spoke and the old man answered and smiled a toothless grin.

"How much is your spirit worth?" the teenager replied.

"I'm only here for another hour, so I really don't have the extra time to spare, maybe some other time," I said, and started to walk away.

"It will take thirty minutes and your payment will be yours to decide once you have completed your journey," the boy spoke for the old man.

"Alright," I said. The old man nodded and pulled forth a pouch of beaded hide and removed a pinch of crushed leaves. He rubbed the earthly gruel between his weathered palms over a clay cup while the boy added water and then he passed the native potion to me.

"What is this stuff," I asked the boy.

"Aruaplsa grass and other herbs made into a tea, it will help you to let go of your inner voice so grandfather can guide you into the mirror world."

"Mirror world?"

"That place where the voice inside of us speaks," he said, and the old man motioned with his hand. "Drink up and then go inside the sweat lodge, and when you exit, you will know what you face and what must be done to correct it. This is the same ceremony that our Navajo warriors preformed when they returned from the Second World War."

I drank and pulled aside the lodge's flap and stepped inside as the old man held onto my shoulder with his ancient claw as if he were divesting all that I was. I felt light and other people were in that dark place, sitting in a ring about the enclosure like faeries from a forgotten experience now reborn of darkness.

"Who are they", I asked, but no answer was given as the drug began to pull me deeper into a place I resisted.

We got fresh faces nine months into our second thirteen-month deployment. Cherries or newbies, we called them, untried and wide-

eyed kids replacing the ones who earned a one way ticket home—the ones the Marines shipped to grieving parents in shiny metal boxes draped with a flag, Stars and stripes shrouding the dead husk of their sorrow.

That was the day Spook came to our unit.

He was a big New Yorker and green Irish to the bone, street tough and sporting a savvy foul mouth that came from the piss-smelling back alleys of Hell's Kitchen. Mark O'Connell had a big head and a wide grin that hid his desire to kill, that Marine installed skill yet to be tested but eager in its anticipation. Sergeant Johnson said he was a spooky-looking fucker, so the combat name 'Spook' stuck.

The appointed Iraqi Governing Council had criticized our unit that month for unnecessary civilian causalities in Al-Fallujah. 'Indiscriminate' was the term they used and the press on both sides ate that shit up.

Sergeant Johnson laughed at their government rhetoric, "This doesn't change a goddamn thing, men. If those cocksuckers shoot at us and run for cover inside a building, unless the occupants push their sorry asses back outside, then every motherfucker in there is a bad guy and our job is to kill the bad guys. Do you prophets of ruin understand me?"

"Sir, yes sir!" the entire platoon sounded off as onc.

"Commit and execute, gentleman, that's the devil dog way. Everyone needs to draw ammo and mount the hummers. Squad leaders, check your men and make sure they're squared away. We're pulling another meat grinder patrol today."

The meat grinder was a catchy little term that told you what it was. Going door to door looking for weapons and bad guys in a city where everyone was considered a bad guy. Just another day of being scared shitless while trying not to show it, another day of getting shot at from who-the-fuck-knows-where, and another day of death on both sides.

Just another day in Johnson's paradise.

Spook had his jaw plugged with fireballs. While most guys in the platoon enjoyed a dip of snuff, Spook liked the hot candy. "Makes you look like you got a jaw full of nuts, you spooky look'n bastard," Johnson would taunt the big-headed kid.

Spook would laugh with the rest of us and spit a sugary red stream, "At least it keeps my mouth moist without looking like I got my gums packed with worm shit." He'd mutter the words under his breath, just loud enough to draw a few snickers from those around him, but soft enough to fall deaf on Johnson's ears. Never piss Johnson off. That was his rule and we lived it.

Half the platoon went about the task of kicking the doors in and clearing the inside while the other half stayed outside providing cover. Curious crowds gathered to watch the action from a distance, waiting to see what happened next. The crowds made you nervous. Tense. They were nothing more than ghoul seekers waiting and watching for the ghastly deeds done by ghastlier men.

A group of kids stood across the road yelling, "America good" to us, waving and holding up peace signs, two dirty fingers tarnishing the air of their pagan God's land. Spook pulled a handful of fireballs from his cargo pocket and started across the street in what Johnson called the zoo effect. These people were animals to him and he made damn sure they were animals to us. Spook was just new enough to still consider them human.

"Don't feed the goddamn animals," Johnson would curse at any man offering food to the children. "Feed the little crumb snatching fuckers and they'll follow you home like a stray. Keep 'em hungry and they'll stay the fuck where they are."

Spook was half way across the street when we heard the single crack of gunfire. Fingers went to triggers, thumbs applying pressure to safeties while vigilant eyes searched the building across the street. Spook was down with Johnson and the corpsman hurtling towards his unmoving body.

Johnson was cussing with every stride, "Goddammit, how many fucking times do I gotta tell you devil dogs to stay in formation, cover your sector, and never feed the motherfucking animals?"

I was crouched behind a charred car and could see the blood spurting from Spook's neck, red spires of death staining the sand in weakening spumes, gurgling breaths coughing crimson to the tune of his blood vomited last words. Then nothing, save the slow gravity trickles of oxygenated pinkish foam. Johnson kneeled and pulled the dog tags from his neck and spun them on a finger, then waved the rest of us over. I didn't want to leave my position. I knew what was lying on the ground between Johnson and the corpsman. Another life gone in this sandbox that demanded our reprisal, and another set of dog tags spinning on Johnson's finger that served as our never-ending reminder.

Johnson had summed up the war best when he'd said, "We're here to kick their ass and take their gas. Democracy's cheap, but oil costs billions. Blood and oil go hand in hand like vodka and orange juice because one compliments the other without the bitter aftertaste."

Johnson directed me with a hand signal to cover the door, "Any sumbitch that comes out that goddamn door, you put a burst into their ass, Judah."

"Roger that, sergeant."

I could see Spook's ashen gray face, jaw still stuffed with fireballs, hand clutching the wrapped candy like they were his bargaining chip out of death. Johnson pulled the black body bag from his ruck and told the corpsman to bag him and called the rest of the platoon to the door I covered. While Johnson and the medic were talking, I picked up one of Spook's fireballs and shoved it in my pocket. I don't know why, I hated that spicy cinnamon candy.

"Did the shot come from this building?" Johnson asked us.

Everyone started talking at once, pointing upstairs, unknowingly condemning the inside dwellers to their fate. Wrong place at the wrong time can cost you. We only wanted justice for Spook, and Johnson was going to make sure we had it.

Johnson took a position to kick in the door, "Judah, Danko, and Pitman, follow me. The rest of you split up and cover the front and back."

The inside smelled like all the rest of the shelled buildings. A musty desertion of an empty attic opened after years of neglect. Shuffling footsteps coming from upstairs got Johnson whispering into his radio, directing the men outside with harsh orders and the men inside with hand signals and tight lips. Danko was working his way up the staircase when a door slammed on the second floor. Johnson held up a fist that halted movement and then gave Pitman a signal to throw a M67 fragmentation grenade. From that day forward, Pitman was known as 'Frag'. It was efficiency at its finest. Speed, surprise and violence of action. It was like a Broadway play rehearsal for the big opening night, except here, a mistake meant a life.

Spook had found that out.

The grenade exploded and extinguished that musty smell replacing it with the coppery scent of blood and cordite. I was moving up the stairs behind Pitman, thinking of Robert Duvall's character in 'Apocalypse Now' shouting, "I love the smell of napalm in the morning."

I loved the smell of cordite and blood in the cramped enclosures. It smelled the same way to me as napalm did to Colonel Kilgore: it smelled like victory.

One body went down at the top of the stairs with legs shattered from the metal fragments sent burning through flesh and bone. He was struggling to rise, searching the floor on his hands and knees for his weapon in the dust motes and smoke. Blind eyes and bloody hands stroking the floor, awaiting the fate he had conjured for all by firing a solitary round. Pitman shot him twice in the head and kept moving while Danko, Johnson, and I covered the rear.

The door on the second floor was locked, but we could hear muffled voices coming from the other side. Johnson gave Pitman the order to cook off another grenade and bounce it inside once Danko kicked the door in. I didn't like cooking off grenades, pulling the pin, letting the spoon fly, and counting to three, which left a few precious seconds before the grenade detonated. It unnerved me. At the mental count of three, you threw it inside like it was a hot coal burning your hand, making sure to bounce it off the floor so the bad guys couldn't pick it up and throw it back at you.

The concussion rocked the entire second floor sending shards of mortar and particles of dirt through the cracks of those ruined walls. Time stops when you burst through a door not knowing who or what is on the other side. We were a mad rush of bodies with weapons at the ready, precious prophets of ruin moving in synchronized rhythms and always shooting at shadows.

A man was writhing about on the floor while an old woman wailed over his broken body. Their clothes were burnt with hundreds of tiny holes oozing blood, still smoking in spots, their eyes listless and their ears deaf due to the concussive blast they'd just endured. Johnson was screaming into the radio, calling for the translator to get his ass upstairs and telling the rest of us to stay clear of the windows lest one of our own might bust a cap in our ass. It happens in that adrenaline fueled haze of battle, friendly fire.

The translator came through the door with our corpsman, we had dubbed our Iraqi translator Gunga Din because it was easier to say and remember than his real name. The old woman fell across the man's body, wailing some foreign name over and over. Her ears were bleeding from ruptured ear drums and the man now lay unmoving, eyes opened and unblinking with his interrupted smile now gracing Allah's palace.

"Tell that raghead cunt to shut the fuck up, Gunga Din. I can't hear the fucking radio with all that crying and shit!" Johnson yelled at the translator.

"She'll be dead before we get her medavac'd out of this shithole, sergeant," the corpsman said, checking her vitals. "She took a lot of shrapnel in her upper body, internal bleeding..." the woman's screams cut the corpsman off when he tried to further examine her.

"Goddammit I said shut that Haji bitch THE FUCK UP!" Johnson screamed.

The translator knelt and spoke softly to the woman, who sobbed and answered back. "She said a man ran inside with a gun and shot from her doorway. Her and her husband told him to leave, but he forced them upstairs and locked them in this room," Gunga Din answered with a thick accent.

"Well, they shoulda done a better job of convincing him to leave," Johnson snapped.

Pitman started laughing and pointing above my head. I turned and looked over my shoulder.

Hanging on the wall was a picture of President Bush and below his grinning face hung an American flag.

"Well fuck me to tears," Danko laughed.

I opened a lot of doors that day to witness what lived and died behind them, and now those locked and guarded doors would haunt me forever.

"I'm blind," I said.

"Open your eyes and drink this," the teenage boy spoke. I was back outside the lodge and the old man sat as he had before with that odd parrot clutching his bony shoulder.

"What is it?" I asked, squinting, my odd colored eye twitched as if it answered to another life on another plane.

"Water, it will help to purge the medicine from your system."

"I don't remember coming back out of the lodge," I said. The boy smiled and the old man chattered away in his native tongue.

"You did not go into the lodge. Grandfather said something inside of you resisted, and until you quench the thirst of this world, you are forbidden to drink from the one beyond."

The bus coughed to life and passengers filed up the steps, I pulled a hundred dollar bill from my wallet and stuck it in the old man's hand.

His benign eyes looked skyward and he spoke as his nappy head wove a tune only the blind could hear. "What did he say?" I asked.

The boy shrugged, "Sometimes grandfather talks in the tongues and only he knows what it means." The old man pulled the boy close to him and whispered in his ear and put something in his hand. "He said for you to take this, it will guard you from what you cannot fight," the teenager explained, and handed me a queer looking stone of black suspended on a woven cord of horse hair.

"Thanks," I said as the driver yelled to all that the bus was leaving. I started trotting across the dusty lot and the boy called after me.

"Make sure you wear that necklace at all times, it's powerful medicine and it won't protect you unless it's around your neck."

PART Six: The Prophets of War

Revelations

"The killer awoke before dawn, he put his boots on."

Jim Morrison

The gathering sky seemed almost divided by the Rocky Mountains as clouds swam by those high and sharpened peaks like whitecaps across a blue-stitched chaparral. The visions and voices I had experienced through the old man's medicine were unnerving, and it forced my psych down another peg on his perceived totem pole of blessings. The bus sped past an old barn with a rusty tin roof that was once used as an improvised billboard: "Buy War Bonds" the faded sign read...

"You wanted to see me sir?" Captain Benson nodded and gestured with his hand toward a chair.

"Please sit down, Corporal Judah. I only want to ask you a few questions and try to ascertain your thoughts on this war." I took the offered chair and gave the good doctor a curt smile.

"Peace is drawn from the blueprints of war, sir."

"Spoken like a true Marine, but is it really that simple, Corporal Judah?" Benson asked, tapping a finger to his chin.

"I overheard what you told Sergeant Johnson about me yesterday behind the latrine," I said, catching him off guard. He leaned back in his chair.

"Did what I say to Sergeant Johnson surprise you?" he asked thinly.

"You think I am some kind of a monster when I am anything but."

He shook his head. "That was wrong of me to say and I apologize, but I am sure you understand that Sergeant Johnson is a hard man to communicate with and unfortunately I let him pull me down to a level I regret.."

"Sir, I've seen more horrors in this war than you could possibly know, and unless you have shared in that conflict, you have no right to label me as anything but a soldier doing his job. You have no right to judge me but you do so anyway because you see the human animal instead of a combat effective Marine. It is impossible for me to find the words to describe what is necessary to survive in a fire fight. Death and terror become your new friends, and war forces you to bond with that realization while they continue to thrive in the twisted wreckage of your memories. There is a part of me that wants to forget and there is another part of me that wants those memories to live. That is my dilemma, and once you distill that knowledge down… there is some kind of morbid genius to it."

"Why?"

"Because there is no morality or standards on either side of this war and the men who create and adapt to the new rules of combat will conquer and survive. That's the way of the Goat, sir."

"Goat?"

"It's our platoon's combat nickname for Sergeant Johnson, sir."

"And that's the only recourse you see, Corporal Judah? To conquer and survive this war by adapting to the rules of the Goat?" Benson *asked and clasped his hands as if in prayer.*

"Pick up a weapon and go with us on our combat patrols. Follow us into the deceit and smoke and face the same demonic smiles we see every day. Do that and you will find out it is as simple as my explanation and as complex as the prophets of ruin who share in that orgy of understanding."

"Corporal Judah, do you think I am sitting here in judgment of you?"

"Your judgment defeats my purpose, sir."

I snapped out of my narcoleptic drone and looked up to see the woman from the truck stop in the aisle staring down at me. She seemed to wear the day's travels in her eyes, honest and mile-soaked without the made up overtones. "I'm sorry about earlier," she apologized and gave me her name. "I'm Jessica Spire."

"Sorry about what?"

"The fight you got in. I feel responsible because I should have just ignored those men and moved to another table. I wanted to apologize earlier, but every time I looked back, you were asleep," she explained. "May I sit down?" I shrugged and scooted to the window seat.

"Please do."

"I didn't catch your name," she smiled and offered her hand.

"I'm sorry, Tom Judah." We shook, her thin hand both dry and warm.

"You made quite an impression at the restaurant, Tom." The sudden bluntness of her observation made me uncomfortable.

"I was actually just trying to be polite because I didn't think those men calling you a bitch was proper, given the circumstances."

"I can honestly say you have a mean ass way of showing polite," she laughed and my edginess subsided. I smiled.

"I've had some practice, Jessica."

"I take it you have a nasty temper."

"Only when I get mad," I replied and looked out the window.

"You don't like these questions, do you?" she asked, staring at me. I turned and stared back. She held my gaze unafraid, almost defiant.

"It's not that," I sighed and rubbed my face. "Look, I can't go back and change what happened at the truck stop, even if I wanted to. I'm sorry if that sounds harsh, but I haven't gotten a lot of sleep the past few days and I'm a little edgy."

"Go ahead and grab some shut eye and I'll come back and wake you up when we get to Denver." Jessica got up and walked back up the aisle, the driver watching us through the mirror. She turned around, "I almost forgot to ask, where are you from?"

"Virginia."

"Me, too," she paused for a second. "If you wake up before we get to Denver, I'll come back and we can talk a bit more if you'd like." I said okay and pulled the blanket over my head to avoid any further conversation.

"Tom?" I blinked and looked up at Jessica Spire's smiling face. The sun broke the background and the hazy light gave her outline a uric halo, like an angel sent forth from one private Heaven to void another. "We're here and the driver said Denver has the Cherry Creek Art Festival going on about two blocks down. We have three hours to kill so I thought maybe we could check it out and grab some food?"

"Yeah, I'm game." I rubbed my face and stood, shouldering my rucksack when my road numb legs buckled, sending me into Jessica.

"Walk it off, big guy," she chided looking at my face and then squinted. "You have the most unusual eyes, is that a contact lens you're wearing?"

"No, it's a birth defect I was born with called heterochromia."

"I've never seen eyes like yours before, they're beautiful."

"My mother used to tell everyone that my eye was kissed by an angel."

"She was right," Jessica said and started up the aisle, then turned back. "You're coming with me aren't you?"

"Yeah, I'm sick of seeing the inside of this bus." I looked down at the seat and saw the necklace the old Indian had given me—it seemed to pulsate with a life force of its own. I picked the crude talisman up and tied the braided horse hair twine around my neck.

Most of the festival goers were dressed casually, while bands of Native Americans danced about in the costumes and decorations of their forebears. Women wore colored sashes tied about their waist while men were adorned in simple buckskin breeches and moccasins. It seemed as if time had turned back and a lost civilization of aborigines were now reborn in living tattooed flesh.

A row of tents let loose the aroma of regional food that was either steaming, roasting, or broiling, and people passed by with plates stacked with meat ranging from chicken to pork. The shaded grass lay stained with lounging bodies and discarded white napkins, like some horrible war had taken place and the wounded lay amid clumps of alien snow that was somehow impervious to the thick and humid air. I was famished. I'd become so engrossed by the beauty and elegance of the festival that I'd forgotten about food or the growing amount of people. The crowd had intensified and people either bumped or nudged me aside if I stopped moving. I didn't like people touching me and I didn't like the crowds or the smell of quartered humanity moving en masse. I was sweating again. Jessica and I had gotten separated and I stood staring straight ahead, food on my mind from another place and time…

It was a Saturday and we were sitting around on our bunks drinking warm beer and eating cans of beans and franks slathered with hot sauce —just old men in our twenty's exchanging lies about what we'd do once the war ended.

"No bastard ever won a war by dying for his country. He won it by making the other poor dumb bastard die for his country. That's how you win a war." Danko did his best General Patton impersonation. Everyone laughed and raised their beers in a toast to ole "Blood and Guts."

Everyone except Sergeant Johnson.

"This war is actually pretty simple… Kill the camel fucker before he kills you," Johnson countered with a shrug.

"That's the way of the Goat," I said. Johnson looked at me and winked.

"How do you think we should handle this war, Sergeant Johnson?" asked Danko.

The tent went quiet.

Johnson took a swig of beer and lit a cigarette. "You want me to tell you how to end this fucking war? Starve these sandal-wearing camel molesters. You can't eat oil or grow anything with it, so if they wanna eat, they can trade oil for food. That pussy Clinton convinced the

United Nations to try this once, but we were too damned good-hearted about it. As soon as CNN and Fox started running blurbs showing swollen bellies and flies buzzing around the camel-jockey kids with infected eyes, we let our hearts decide. The problem with this war is the media is letting the people back home decide what goes on here. Everyone was patriotic and quick to fight after September 11th, but as soon as the blood started flowing, they wanna call it quits before our job is done. Do you devil dogs know what the people did when they showed news reels at the movies when we fought in World War Two?"

No one spoke.

Johnson grinned and exhaled twin plumes of smoke from his nose like some degenerate and fiendish clown. "They fucking cheered every time the screen flashed a dead Jap some flamethrower had burnt to a hideous, gook carcass. Do you honestly think the people are cheering over what they show on the nightly news back home? These godless fucks over here are heartless demons and we gotta be the heartless prophets of ruin. We're gonna rule their miserable world and if they don't want to play ball our way, then they're gonna pay in fucking flesh. Let us do the killing and the camera man can film all the sand nigger kids with dead milky eyes they want to." Johnson eyed each man, "Besides, Patton's dead and I'm not and we're gonna play war by my rules this time."

"You'll go straight to hell for thinking that way," Danko laughed.

"There'll be a lot of devil dogs there waiting for the Goat to arrive and if we got to fight Hell's fire... we'll fight it together. Ask yourself,

would these heathen fucks over here give a flying rat's ass if we were starving in the good ole US of A?" Again, no one answered. "I didn't think so. You men might as well get it through your heads and toughen the fuck up because we're here for one purpose. To kill bad guys, period. That's what the good guys do and that's why they sent every fucking one of us over here. We're gonna rid the world of these rag-wearing demons, then go the fuck home happy and tapping our toes to the Star Spangled Banner."

"Are you hungry?" Jessica asked, walking up.

"Yeah, I'd almost forgotten about eating until now. Where were you?" I looked away to hide my sweaty face.

"I love abstract art of any kind and went through a few displays and must've lost you in the crowd. Now that I've found you, let's grab something to eat." Jessica smiled and took my hand.

That simple gesture was cute and casual, like a gentlemanly suggestion of recognition when attending some glitzy formal—it was all for show with no affection. But her hand was different than it was when she introduced herself and we shook on the bus. I knew because it felt warm and dry then… and now it had that same sheen of nervous moisture my own hand held.

A large tent had been erected behind the craft section of the festival, providing shade and comfort to those eating their food. Orderly lines filed past the fare with an eye-sampling pace that reminded me of the chow tent in Iraq. It was the only spot that offered an escape to the killing, a place you went and put the war on pause so you could eat. Both places had that same crunch of Styrofoam being pressed into bags while voices yammered away in the background. But it wasn't the same and neither was I.

"I have absolutely no idea what I'm seeing other than the hot dogs and hamburgers, but most of it looks pretty damned good," I said as we got in line.

"Why don't you grab us a place to sit over in the tent and I'll pick out a couple dishes for us to try?"

"Does this mean I'll be forever in your debt?" I grinned.

"Not if you grab the drinks," she said. "Tea for me."

"Sweetened or unsweetened?"

"Sweetened, of course," She gave me that smile of hers. It made me feel secure when I had no right.

I found an empty table next to a long rectangular fire pit made from stacking cinder blocks together. Chicken wire was stretched lengthwise across the blocks for a grilling surface and next to the crude structure sat an elderly black man basting a variety of wild game before a mixed audience. He seemed to work the homemade grill with some handed down Negro philosophy as he watched the charred skin cracking to the heated embers below. I shivered at some ghastly memory and turned away from the scene.

Jessica sat down and slid a plate with meat and relish across the table to me. "The cook said this was elk, smoked and basted in its own juices, and served with a side of spicy pepper relish and covered with peach chutney."

I raked my fingers through tight napped hair, "I'm afraid if I get any of this meat on my forehead, my tongue would slap my brains out trying to lick the stain."

Jessica started laughing and held a napkin to her mouth, "I've never heard that one before."

"It's a phrase we say around home when you're about to taste something good," I forced a smile.

I shoved a forkful of meat, relish, and chutney into my mouth while Jessica continued to laugh and nearly passed out from the pleasure that first bite gave. Being hungry and having a large appetite adds flavor to the weakest dish, but this needed nothing. The tart pepper relish broke down the gamy taste of the elk and left a smoky goodness that can only take place during cooking. It seemed to tenderize and infuse the meat, allowing the soft peach chutney to cover each bite with sweet perfection.

"What do you think?" Jessica asked.

I held up a hand and continued to chew the first bite until I swallowed. "Damn that's good… real good." I exhaled and took a sip of tea.

Jessica smiled. "I'm glad you like it."

We ate and watched a contest of Native American skills being displayed by men of all ages. I liked the thought of that brand of competition, a crowning of the manliest man to rule their fictional and abolished realm for a year. It's too bad wars and political differences couldn't be settled this way. Let the world take the Presidents and square them off against the Kings and Dictators in an inter-global Olympics. Events would range from bare-knuckle boxing to broadsword duels with the winner controlling the oil and food for a year. But the world isn't ready for that kind of a solution to war. War will always be about old men making the decision to send a country's youth to their death. A spreadsheet of lives expended versus accrued and earthly gains.

There's no glory in that.

We finished our meal and chatted about the festival and watched as tent's audience grew in numbers. In the distance, tribal drums sounded and seemed to vibrate the smoky air in deep echoing rhythms. I was thinking about how they sounded like the impact of distant air strikes when a something behind me popped. I ducked my head and went to a knee while feeling across my chest for the rifle's sling. Old habits now awakened as I knelt, vigilant eyes and nervous fingers ready for action. I looked over my shoulder and shared the same look of shock with a little girl and her deflated balloon hanging limply from her chubby hand.

Those sharp cracks still got to me because you will never shake that devilish bark of gunfire and everyone screaming and pointing at once where it came from. It's funny because as soon as you hear the crack, it's too late to duck, but you jam your head through your shoulders anyway and wonder how close that one came. In the war movies when someone's hit, there's only a trickle of blood and the hero's soft voice talking about a mother's love. There's never any screaming when the movie star dies, no bloody coughs as the hero gently closes his eyes to the solemn faces gathered around.

I wanted war to be like that, but it's not. There's always screaming and blood and there's always complete and utter chaos. Sweat beaded my forehead. I was embarrassed and picked up my napkin then sat back down facing Jessica like a tarnished pervert.

"What's wrong? You're pale as a ghost," she asked while shooing a loom of swarming flies.

"Lost my napkin," I lied and changed the subject. "I almost forgot to ask, what part of Virginia are you from?"

"Stuarts Draft," she said.

"No kidding, I'm from Waynesboro."

"I know where Waynesboro is, it's a small town about fifty miles southwest along the Blue Ridge Mountains. I went hiking there last spring near a church being run by a bunch of snake handlers."

"The snake handling is just a small part of the Pentecostal practice," I explained and looked down at the table. "My Uncle Frank is the preacher of that church."

She started apologizing, "I'm so sorry, Tom. I didn't mean anything by the snake handler remark because religion has always screwed with my head so I've stayed away from it."

"Yeah, it's fucked with my head, too," I said. We laughed and then it was my turn to apologize, "I shouldn't have said that."

"I've heard worse language in my classroom, Tom."

"You go to school?"

She shook her head. "No, I'm a teacher. How about you?"

"I just got out of the military, so I'm not sure. There aren't a lot of options for me, so I'll either go back to school or start bouncing the club scene again."

"You were a bouncer?"

"Yeah, until I reenlisted."

"What will you major in if you decide to go back to school?"

"I was majoring in journalism before I went to Iraq," I said.

"So you quit school to go and fight in the war?"

"Yeah."

"What made you do that, you didn't like school or school didn't like you?" she asked and smiled.

"A little of both I guess." I smiled back as an old Indian man stopped before us and spoke to me in a strange tongue. We sat and listened until he made a sign as if to bless our table and then walked away. Jessica looked at me and shrugged.

"Wonder what he said?" she asked.

A Native American woman beside us pointed at me and explained, "The old one recognized the stone necklace you're wearing and said he wishes you a safe journey."

"Thank you," Jessica answered for me and looked at my necklace. I had forgotten about the talisman the blind Indian had given me and it seemed to pulse around my neck like a foreign heartbeat.

"I wonder what journey he was talking about," Jessica said, looking the crowd over for the old man. I shrugged and wondered myself.

"Maybe he was talking about the bus trip we're taking… I dunno."

PART 7: End of the Line

Goodbye Magic Bus

"Reality is a sliding door." Ralph Waldo Emerson

"Hey… Hey, you ignorant asshole, you're gonna wake my kid up."

I opened my eyes and looked across the aisle at a boy snuggled against his redneck mother like he was suckling her teat. "I'm sorry, was I talking in my sleep?" I apologized. Jessica Spire stirred sleepily in the seat beside me.

"Hell no, you musta been having a bad dream cause you were jerking all over the place, you stupid prick." The woman said it with her best crackhead grimace before moving to an unoccupied section near the front of the bus. The driver's eyes pierced the rearview mirror, watching me as a road sign blinked by my window: "Welcome to Nebraska, Equality before the Law" the sign had read.

I yoked an arm behind my back as the sun began to ride the morning sky like a blistering orb sent from some higher humanity. I stared through the tinted window at that fiery ring, remembering something odd my dad and Uncle Frank used to do on Sunday evenings after we'd received the Gospel. They'd sit outside in the shade of our walnut tree snapping dinner beans while chanting the same line of a song over and over. It was the chorus to 'Ring of Fire' and I knew then that the malignancy of my mind had slipped down another cancerous notch. I couldn't remember why, but I hated this song for some reason.

Jessica cracked an eye open. "Jesus, what the hell got into her? Everyone has a bad dream from time to time."

"Even you?"

"Even me what?"

"Have bad dreams," I asked.

"The only bad dream I have is seeing my ex-husband coming at me with his hands open and choking me unconscious. When I came to, he was crying because he thought I was dead, and the thing that always got me was... he never once tried to revive me or call for help."

"What happens when you wake up?"

"I file for divorce and when the papers are served, I sneak off to Salt Lake City to stay with my college roommate for the summer." She forced a smile.

"Why didn't you fly?"

"I'm scared to death of flying," she said and laughed. "How about you?"

"I got married a month before I left for Iraq and divorced a year later when I came back home."

"I didn't mean that, I meant your bad dreams."

"Just bad shit," I said, shaking my head.

"Bad shit like what we see about the war on the news?"

"There's a difference in what *you* see and what I've seen, Jessica. You see the twisted carnage and the broken bodies while the anchorman is talking above the wailing and sirens. When you are there in the moment, you smell the feces and the diesel and the burning flesh. You can almost taste the cracked and crumbling world around you and it's in that closeness of it all, being there in the real time and having your mind try to deal with that sudden sensory overload. It gives your dreams an actual odor that you can never really hide from."

We made the six hour route to Indianapolis while I stayed handcuffed to my yoked arm and faked sleep, then transferred to another bus bound for Charleston, West Virginia.

"Can I ask you something if you promise you won't let it piss you off?" Jessica asked and clutched her knees to her chest.

"Go ahead."

"You said you were a bouncer for a while, why?"

I shrugged and replied, "I was good at it."

"You were good at it or," she paused and looked at me unsure.

"Or what?"

"Never mind, I'm afraid you're going to get pissed if I ask," she said shaking her head.

"I'm not pissed, Jessica. Go ahead and say what's on your mind."

She took a deep breath and exhaled. "Or was it because you liked it? I only say that because I saw the way your face changed when you got in that fight, it's the same look my ex-husband had when he was drunk, but with you there was a difference…"

"I was sober?" I cut her off.

"Yeah," Jessica said the word as if she were embarrassed by its finality. "The abuse always bothered him once the alcohol wore off, but the violence doesn't seem to affect you."

"I don't think about the pain and brutality when it happens, I learned to deal with that side of violence first and worry about my conscience later."

"And that's what made you good at it?"

"I don't know how to explain it much more than that without sounding elitist; it would be like asking a pitcher to describe how he can throw a baseball faster than anyone else in the league."

"The fight you had back at the restaurant, you knew exactly what to do and it was over with in the blink of an eye... How did you know which way to react?" she asked, leaning forward.

"I worked for an old bouncer I called Mighty Mike at my first club and he sorta took me in under his wing. We worked out with weights together before our gigs and he taught me to throw a punch and how to use every part of my body as a weapon. He was a people watcher and because of that, he could spot a trouble maker before the guy downed his first beer of the night. He used to tell me you had to decide in life whether or not you wanted to be a good guy or a bad guy."

"What's the difference to a bouncer, Tom?"

"A good guy is someone people want to be around because they know he is a man you can trust, someone to turn to when the chips are down."

"And a bad guy?"

"Mike used to say a bad guy will never earn any respect and will likely live out his life having to watch his back because no one else will do it for him." Talking about violence got me excited. I paused and looked at her.

"Go ahead, Tom. This is fascinating."

"Mike told me that first night I worked for him that there were two types of men I'd face in the bouncer business: the good guys were the men who had no need to be in a fight and never felt the brutal crunch of knuckles meeting flesh."

"And the other type?" she asked.

"The bad guys were the men who have been knocked down but keep getting back up. It pays to know what kind of man you're facing and you learn to distinguish between the two by watching them, understanding those subtle traits all men have and hide so well. Things like if they are right handed or left handed, how they deal with you in a confrontation, and where their hands are held while they're talking. You put this together in a matter of seconds and then you watch and wait."

"Wait?"

"You watch and wait for him to let his guard down and give you an opening to attack. It could be the shift of his attention to a friend, taking his eyes off you, or slightly relaxing his posture. And when that hesitation occurs, you counter with speed and an all consuming violence of action until the threat is neutralized."

"At the restaurant, you only fought two of the three men, but you seemed to have already pegged which two of the guys was trouble," she said. I nodded.

"The one that called you a bitch," I started. She interrupted.

"The pretty boy?"

"Yeah, well pretty boy had manicured fingers and smooth yoga arms that had seen a few too many hours basting in a tanning bed. He likely came from a wealthy background and used his family's money as a trump card. That told me pretty boy was nothing more than a loud mouth talker with two friends for backup. The guy closest to him stayed by his shoulder and asked him to leave, so I knew he wasn't ready to fight. The other clown I outweighed by fifty pounds and he stayed ten feet away from his two friends. Pretty boy was right handed and when he started to say something smartass, he hesitated and that pause gave me the opening I needed, so I capitalized on that advantage. When I took him down, the runt ran and his other friend just stood there; that reluctance to fight left him vulnerable so I kicked his ass for being stupid enough to hang out with assholes."

"Amazing," she said and looked at me unsmiling. "And your conscience doesn't bother you at all?"

"My conscience is intact," I lied and stretched.

"Whatever happened to the old bouncer you worked for?"

"Mighty Mike?" She nodded and shifted in her seat. "He was stabbed to death in a club near Memphis while I was in Iraq serving a second combat tour of duty."

"Jesus, Tom... I'm sorry," Jessica said, spotting my tattoo and quickly changed the subject. "What does your tattoo mean?"

I pointed to the horned bulldog. "I was a Marine and Marines are known as devil dogs, The Prophets of Ruin was the nickname given to my platoon. The circle on the dog's head with the plus sign on the inside of it stands for O-Positive, my blood type," I explained.

"The words below the dog, what do they mean?"

"*Cave Canem...* It's Latin for Beware of the Dog," I said, pulling my sleeve down and taking out my iPod.

"What kinds of music do you download?"

"Pretty much everything," I said, looking down at the player. "A buddy of mine used to say that an iPod made a slave of the listener, but the music is what truly captured the soul."

"What did that mean?"

"I dunno, Jessica... I must be tired because I can't even remember his name for some reason."

"You miss it, don't you?"

"Miss what?"

"The military," she said.

"It's weird, it's almost like I was raped for three years and instead of hating it... you find out a small part of you secretly liked what was happening."

"There's nothing to like about rape," Jessica answered, looking away. Her tone was different and her voice had a harder edge to it.

"I didn't exactly mean it in that context. I don't miss the rules but I miss the men that I served with. You share so much hardship together that you come to not only know them, but in an odd way, you learn to love these men more than any person in your life. You believe in your buddies and they believe in you and you are proud to be a part of that bond. I dunno, it's hard to find the right words to explain it unless you were there and lived that kind of life," I answered and closed my eyes to avoid any more questions. "Wake me up when we get to the West Virginia state line.

My explanation seemed to relax Jessica's edge. "Sweet dreams," she replied.

The aluminum boxes were stacked in rows three wide on the floor of a C-141. All the hopes and dreams that once breathed life now reduced to these coffered symbols, reminders and memories under the flag-draped husk we were sending home as ghosts of Iraqi freedom. I was saying good-bye to Frag. We were all given one word nicknames by Johnson to depersonalize death, and Pitman had become 'Frag' the same day he'd become one of The Prophets of Ruin.

He was driving the Hummer and I was sitting in the passenger seat talking about chicks and home. We were just a couple Marines sharing a part of their lives, harmless prom night lies and bullshit 'when I get back home' stories. It was our way of making the Prophets of Ruin almost human by trading youthful dreams we kept alive by staying alive. Create the brotherly bond, that's the devil dog way.

Frag was humming 'Ring of Fire' by Johnny Cash when the IED detonated behind the driver's seat and split our Hummer down the middle. I sensed things in choppy, stepwise chunks. The acrid smell of burning rubber and flesh. Frag's severed foot pressing the brake as my burning iPod was blown out of my hand and instantly melted to his boot. The rest of him was gone from the waist down. Everything that he was disappeared in a flash of fire and smoke. I took Frag's iPod off his smoldering flak vest and stuck it in my pocket, then stumbled from the door, bleeding from my ears. Hearing temporarily ruptured. Tone deaf and numb to the screaming and fighting, strange hands pushing me to the ground and the corpsman talking while Sergeant Johnson was yelling directions through the haze... Blackness.

That was the day I began to forget the more important tangents of my life. It was the day I finally earned my Prophets of Ruin nickname and Johnson began calling me Lazarus. When I regained consciousness at the field hospital, I saw the faces of death for the first time, as if I was guilty and condemned thereafter for the resurrection I stole without their consent.

"What did you lose?" I heard Jessica's voice.

I snapped awake with my head buried between the seatbacks and my hand scrabbling the floor to my front. My fingers clutched the fallen

MP3 player and I sat upright both sweaty and misguided. "I dropped my iPod," I said.

"I was getting ready to wake you up anyway, the transmission went out two hours ago and a shuttle bus is going to pick us up and take us to a hotel for the night. The driver said Greyhound is paying for the room and our meals," she explained. I looked around at the rustle of passengers spilling into the aisle amid the blaring light from a smaller bus, the people gathered around me like those of shadow things playing with the minds of lesser men.

"Let's get the hell off this thing," I said and stood. "We have one more transfer in Charleston and we'll finally be headed home."

"Not for me," Jessica replied.

"Why's that?"

"I parked my car at the Charleston terminal and caught a bus from there. I knew that once my ex-husband couldn't find me or my car, he'd give up looking for me after a week and I wanted to keep it that way."

"He's that bad?" I asked, blocking the crowd and letting her duck into the aisle.

"Pretty bad," she answered and turned around. "Why don't you ride the rest of the way home with me? I could use the conversation and I wouldn't have to worry about you fighting bad dreams and scaring off the passengers."

"Yeah, that sounds good. I'll see if I can cash in the rest of my ticket and I'll fill your car up with gas." couldn't remember why.

The motor lodge was a ramshackle structure sprung up beside a faded and forgotten access road, barren memories silent on the interior walls where the closets hid more than the dust of its coldly-written memoirs. We filed into the lobby and across the putting green indoor/outdoor carpet to the Formica counter. Jessica was humming a song and I was lost in its name as the check-in line moved forward a step. Onward Christian Soldiers was the tune and the oddity of her selection did not escape me.

"You get the dinner special at the diner next door and one beverage of your choice, non-alcoholic," the hotel man said with a rehearsed cadence. "Tomorrow morning we have a small continental breakfast from 6am to 8am and the bus leaves at 8:15. So I would appreciate it if all checkouts were done before you eat." I nodded and was given room 13A. "Also," the man added. "I'll need to hold either a credit card or your driver's license until you checkout."

"Why?" I asked.

"We've had some guests get a little reckless with our furniture in the past."

I handed him my license and Jessica requested the room adjacent to mine. "We're separate but traveling together," she explained.

The man looked at her and grinned, his hair a clownish wig of some greasy product and smoothed like seamless plastic against his pipered skull. The thin smile he wore at her simple request had betrayed past lovers and the anti-blessings of their deceit. He was still grinning at Jessica like a peephole fiend. "Sure, but the same rules apply to you and only one occupant to a room," he said, handing over the key to room 13B.

"Thanks Elvis," Jessica said, mocking the clerk's hair style and gave the man a two-fingered salute. I smiled at the comment and followed her through swinging glass doors to the chipped patio. "We're on the second floor," she said, extending the suitcase handle and pulling her bag up a set of concrete stairs.

"I would have gotten that for you," I told her. She turned left at the top and stopped at her room.

"I'm used to it," she replied, then turned the key and opened the door.

"Is your conscience bothering you?" I asked, passing by her open door.

She stepped into the room and stuck her head back outside like a puppet. "What's this about my conscience?"

"That crack you made about the clerk's hair downstairs, didn't making fun of him bother your conscience the least little bit?" I asked and grinned.

"He was being an asshole and don't worry about me, my conscience is perfectly intact," she replied and ducked back inside. I stepped into my room where the musty stench of infrequent use seemed to eat at the walls. "Hey, can you hear me?" Jessica yelled through the petition of plaster separating us.

"Yeah."

"After you get cleaned up, come and get me and we'll grab something to eat."

I wasn't really hungry, but I was beginning to enjoy her company. "Alright," I yelled back. "Give me an hour to shower and change."

"It's a date."

I showered and changed into jeans and a tee shirt, then dropped back on the bed. The curtains were at half mast and I watched as passengers pulled their bags up the staircase. I flinched and blinked each time those plastic wheels clopped a pittance against the concrete rungs. I yawned and slipped back to that museum of memories I no longer controlled...

My platoon had lost three guys that June. Three men I knew. Three men I'd shared laughs with over the bland food they served for chow. I saw them die that morning when an RPG smashed through their convoy truck. I knew the men inside were dead before we pulled the charred remains from the wreckage. These were my friends, buddies with black charcoal faces now smoldering like burnt remnants of a dark and lifeless hearth.

Sergeant Johnson said it best: "There's no time for good-byes in war, only hello to what happens after it."

I dismounted my Humvee and ran to a point to provide security as the rounds snapped the sand around those of us who remained. We stumbled like bloodied zombies flailing through an intersection where the rooftop Haji's popped caps from their high-ground advantage. I pushed my face deeper into the sand, not wanting to get hit it the head while rounds bore into that grainy world around me. It's a funny thing about getting shot when one bullet to the head ends the suffering quickly, painlessly, but the fear of dying that way scared you more than getting hit someplace else. At least getting hit somewhere else left you a chance. It might hurt like hell, but you weren't dead. You don't think about dying before you see combat, nobody does. It's the cocky naivety of youth that vanishes when you taste what war has to offer. It changes you forever. We became old men behind the faces of boys... everyone except Elvis. His face would never change from that day forward.

Cedric Filson came fresh from Boston and loved three things in his short, violent life. The Red Sox, his turret mounted .50 caliber machine gun he named 'the King,' and Elvis Presley. Johnson dubbed Filson 'Elvis,' and each time Filson made a kill, he'd shout down to the driver from his gunner's perch..."Hail to the King, baby." He was a dumbass kid who bought into the thrill ride of combat fire fights and even had his family send him a pair of replica glasses like the originals his namesake wore.

Elvis had his .50 caliber methodically dismantling the buildings to the front with the steady thump, thump, thump, of the large rounds. Dust covered everything, creating a battle of ghostly apparitions darting from cover to cover like beings baptized in smoke and gloom. I was scared, biting my lip to hold back the fear with my head buried in the sand. You find there's a lot more to God in that gritty wasteland when *you're face down among it, the air pushing from your mouth in ragged puffs creating small craters—you're that close to the ground. Elvis swung his weapon to the left and then brutally lurched forward, his glasses falling and landing next to my knee. I picked them up and blew the dust off the scratched lenses and looked up, expecting Elvis to snatch them from my hand and say something smartass. His teeth hit me in the face.*

From his nose to his chin was gone and bloody spit gurgles came out instead of words as his eyes blinked violently. Rags of pasty meat hung and fluttered like bloody banners from his half-headed body. I tucked his glasses down my shirt as Johnson screamed at the driver to skin the fuck out of that location, taking Elvis's bobbing corpse swaying with each turn as they sped to the rear of our column.

There was a knock at my door. I shivered as my mind stumbled back from those dark and deserted days. "Hey, are you ready to go?" Jessica asked.

PART Eight: One Night

Almost Heaven

"All men dream but not equally. Those who dream by night in the dusty recesses of their minds wake in the day to find that it was vanity: but the dreamers of the day are dangerous men, for they may act their dream with open eyes to make it possible." T. E. Lawrence

The diner was no more than a grunge hole, catering to the late night carousers and other fine jesters of the dark; matrons scuttled among the disarray of tables and pocketed humanity with a jilted presence and wore the everyday grime of their lives on stained aprons. Old black and white photographs of coal miners littered the putrid walls and were as faded as the nameless faces of those men that now lay buried and forgotten in the kinetic womb of this earth. The waitress working our booth looked at us with dull eyes and blinked away this acoustic shadow of these past enterprises.

"Y'all with the bus that broke down?" she asked, licking the tip of her pencil.

"Yes," Jessica replied. I nodded.

"Tonight's special for the Greyhound passengers is Salisbury steak with gravy and mashed potatoes, two dinner rolls and your choice of ice tea or coffee. If you want anything other than the special or an extra side, you'll have to pay for it out of your own pocket."

"We'll have two specials with tea, one sweetened and one unsweetened," I said.

Jessica took a sip of water while I stared through the grimy window at the mountains that lay scalped by the mining industry like some horrible disaster had robbed them of their crown. I wondered what West Virginia looked like before the coal and timber industry came and raped the land, I wondered what Iraq looked like before twenty tons of explosives dropped from the sky and scarred that land of jaded prophets forever. It didn't matter—a thousand years from now our historians would write with great solidarity that it was a just and noble cause.

"What are you looking at?" Jessica asked. I tilted my head towards the window.

"What's left of those mountains, my father used to tell me there was more history in a pound of mountain soil than all the written records of mankind." Jessica smiled and started to reply when the waitress returned with our plates cradled in one arm and our drinks balanced in the palm of her opposite hand. She clanged the order down, then turned without a word and wandered back through the sluggish air and the mismatched tables, a little deeper into her under appreciated world.

Jessica looked down at her plate and shook her head, "I can't eat this." I looked at our orders, pools of grease swam atop the meat like the gauzy eyes of a dead fish. "Besides, this place is too smoky to even think about eating. You don't smoke do you?" she asked, pinching her nose.

"I did for about six months when I was in Iraq but I quit. Hell, I can't even remember the reason why I started. I hate the smell of cigarettes."

"Me too," she replied and looked around for our waitress. "Why don't we head back to my room and order a pizza if we can find a place that will deliver?" I nodded and chuckled.

"We'll find one. Even in Iraq they had a Pizza Hut that would deliver right to the front door of your billets. The first time I ordered a pizza, I almost shit myself when the delivery guy showed up."

"Why?"

"Because he looked like the people we were fighting except this guy was holding a pizza in one hand and a loaded assault rifle in the other. It blew me away that a job like delivering a pizza required you to carry a loaded weapon," I explained.

"The hell with that," Jessica answered, still looking the crowd over for our waitress. "I wonder if we have to sign a ticket or something before we leave."

"Probably not."

"Then we're outa here," she said, waving a hand through the smoky air and sliding out the booth. As we passed by the checkout counter, the words 'We Deliver' on a sticker caught my eye and I nudged Jessica from behind. She stopped and turned and I pointed to the advertisement. "Perfect," she said, punching the number on her cell phone then listening to the voice giving her their rehearsed cadence of specials. She started giggling.

"What's so funny?" I asked, holding the door for her. We stepped outside and walked back towards the hotel, she cupped the phone and looked at me like we were about to reveal a secret.

"You can order a six pack of beer with your pizza."

"No shit."

"Wanna split one?" she asked.

"Why the hell not."

I stayed in Jessica's room while she hung around the front desk waiting for the food. She lent me her phone to call my father and I thought about waiting a few days, but dialed the number anyway. He answered on the third ring.

"Dad?"

"Tommy, is that you?"

"Yeah, are you busy right now?" I asked.

"Where are you, son? I waited at the airport until they checked the passenger list and told me you weren't on the flight."

"I sent you an e-mail. I fell asleep and missed my plane. I'm at a hotel in West Virginia."

"Why?"

"It's a long story but I took a bus instead of flying and the thing broke down, so Greyhound put the passengers up in a hotel until tomorrow morning."

"Are you coming home, son?" he asked in a tone that seemed to plead.

"Yeah... maybe in a few more days."

"Are you alright, Tommy?"

"Yeah, I'm fine, dad."

"You call me when you get here and I'll come get you. The hospital called and wondered why you haven't checked back in... Son, are you still on the line?" he asked after a pause.

"Yeah." I heard him sigh on the other end.

"Did you hear what I said about the hospital calling?"

"They'll have to wait, dad... I'm kinda tired from the road so I'm gonna grab some sleep. I'll call you in a couple of days."

"Be careful, son."

"I will, dad. Love you."

"I know, son... Good to hear your voice again," he said and hung up.

I closed the phone as Jessica thumped the door open with her foot and backed into the room with our order. She handed me a beer and opened the box, the smell of pepperoni invaded the cramped room like some delicious ghost had been released upon a famine.

"Now this is more like it," she said, closing her eyes and inhaling. I popped open my can and started to drink when she put a hand across my arm. "Wait until I get one open and I'll propose a toast."

"A toast over beer and pizza?" I shook my head in mock disbelief. Jessica laughed and opened a can of beer, then clinked our cans.

"It might be redneck as hell, but here's to travel partners," she said, lifting her can in a mock salute and we drank.

We sat on the bed and ate slices of pizza and drank beer as if we were old chums sharing a feast over some odd adventure planned, but yet to come.

"I guess your parents are proud of you and glad you're home," Jessica said, closing the empty box and wiping her hands.

"My dad is, my mother passed away from diabetes last year."

"I'm sorry, Tom. I lost my mother to cervical cancer when I was thirteen."

"Do you miss her?" I asked. She nodded her head and popped open the last beer. I was feeling the effects of what I had drank, mellow and drowsy. Comfortable. Jessica crossed her legs and swallowed.

"Yeah, but I miss the things we never had a chance to share while I was growing up," she explained.

"Like what?"

"My dad did a good job raising me, but there are things only a mother and daughter can talk about, and my mother wasn't there when I needed that. It made me feel cheated so I kinda rebelled against my dad and found myself married to a man he didn't like, not because I loved him and that was the worst mistake I made in our marriage." She looked at me as if there was something I needed to add.

"It's the same way with me. I was always close to my mom because she was the one person that kept me clean both inside and out. My dad was always a little jealous of how close my mother and I were... it's almost unnatural he used to tell us." I looked at her and she held my stare, looking intently at my half-colored eye. "I don't know why I'm telling you that," I added and dropped my head. She bent over and cocked her head until our faces met like the tease of a first kiss.

"Why are you then?"

"I don't know… maybe because I feel I can trust you," I said with a shrug. She smiled and sat back.

"You're a lot different when you let your guard down," Jessica replied, finishing her beer.

"The Marine counselors said I suppressed and guarded my emotions because I was an 'A-Type' individual." She looked confused and swallowed. "I'm an extreme over achiever," I explained.

"Meaning you don't like to be wrong or lose?"

"It means I crave a perfection that does not exist."

"Perfection does exist," she said, shooting the empty can into the waste basket like a basketball player. I shook my head no.

"Perfection doesn't exist in this world, Jessica."

"I've seen perfect sunsets," she challenged.

"The sunset you see is perfect to you but only when you're in that space of time. But somewhere in the world, the sun will rise and set in the same manner and go unnoticed with the same beauty only you perceived as perfection. There have been millions upon millions of sunsets since the dawn of time, so how could a solitary sunset be seen as perfect?"

"Well, then, Jesus was perfect," she countered. I nodded slightly.

"He was until the cross. Once those nails were driven into his body, it stained the perfection that he was by leaving a blemish. And those three scars tainted that prophet forever and that's why I am the way I am; I try to achieve perfection in everything that I do."

"Like how?" she asked.

"I signed up for the Marines because my father told me they were the best. I was honor grad for my boot camp class and volunteered for the top platoon in the division so I could serve under the most decorated platoon sergeant in the Corps. From that point on, I stayed in some sort of odd and macabre contest with the man for the three tours I served under him."

"What was his name," she asked.

"Sergeant Johnson."

"Why did you get out then?"

"I didn't get out. They sent me home."

"Why?"

"Because one of our division doctors said I wasn't cut out for war. I had already pulled two combat tours and was on my third, and they take a hard look at that kind of individual to see the reason why. I was classified as an A-Type so I was sent back stateside," I explained.

"And you didn't like that," she said.

"No, because I can control my destiny, but I cannot control my fate."

"No one can control destiny, Tom."

"That's what an A-Type individual does, Jessica. They control their destiny."

"How can you control your own destiny?" she asked, shaking her head.

"My mother was a tested and certified genius. At age thirteen, she had one of the highest Mensa test scores ever recorded. She graduated high school at fifteen and was accepted immediately into Harvard where she majored in Theology and Application. She met my father through my Uncle Frank's church when she was exploring the Pentecostal religious practices in Appalachia and never went back to school."

"Why?" Jessica interrupted.

"She fell in love with my dad and the Pentecostal religion and her family broke all ties with her because they were wealthy Irish Catholics from Boston. I guess the thought of their genius daughter living in the mountains and leaving behind a bright future didn't sit to well with them."

"So your mom was an honest to God genius?"

I nodded. "She memorized the Pentecostal Bible in one week and could quote any passage word for word that you gave her. She used to play a game of verse with me while I was growing up to help me memorize the Bible like she had. She would recite a poem and give me a random book and verse, and I would quote it back to her and then I would give her one to recite," I explained.

"And she was never wrong?"

"Not ever."

"What was the poem she used to say?"

I looked at her and quoted:

>*"When you feel life's great cost,*
>*Discouraged and thinking all is lost.*
>*Recite a verse and Angels will descend,*
>*To guide you through your journey's end.*
>*Recite another and your soul will soar,*
>*Keeping your demons behind God's door."*

"That still doesn't explain how you can control destiny," Jessica said and lay back on the bed. I dropped beside her and propped myself up against the head board.

"I do not deviate from a goal... not ever. Once I am given a specific task, I will achieve and I do not accept failure. That is what I cannot control. My destiny is to be the best at any given mission, to exceed all others and become the example ordinary men are measured against. I can control that by working harder to eliminate the possibility of defeat and it is my destiny to be so. Fate is an obstacle I cannot control and Dr. Feelgood said when those two worlds clash, it could send me into an abyss. I never memorized the Bible to the exact details like my mother had, and the good doctor explained that it was because of my mother's relentless push for me to be like her, to memorize every word of every passage—It created an A-Type personality instead of a genius," I answered and blinked back to that conversation...

"I wanted to talk with you so you could hear it from me first," Captain Benson addressed me in his office.

"About what, sir," I replied, taking a seat.

"I plan on asking Sergeant Johnson to send you back to the states again." I looked at him and shrugged. "Why do you think that is necessary from my standpoint, Corporal Judah?" he asked.

"Because you have a fucking hard on for me," I answered and lit a cigarette.

"When did you start smoking?"

"It's a new habit I just picked up." I winked and exhaled smoke through my nose.

"I don't have anything against you, Corporal Judah, but you're split between two opposing worlds and I'm afraid of what might happen when those worlds collide inside your head."

"I have no idea what in the hell you're talking about, sir."

"Part of your A-Type individuality follows the religious teachings of your mother, and the other part of you follows Sergeant Johnson and his renegade doctrine."

I started shaking my head. "No, sir... that's bullshit and you know it. I belong here with the Prophets of Ruin and I will not leave until I have completed my mission."

"Tom, listen to me," he said, rapping his knuckles against the desk. "Right now, those worlds coexist and you're fine, but I think you're beginning an inner fight between religion and the harsh necessities you're using to survive in combat."

"Is that all, sir?" I asked and stood.

"Unless there is something else you want to talk about?" I shook my head and snubbed out the cigarette on my palm. He looked at me and sighed. "You're excused then."

"Thank you, sir." I saluted and turned to leave when his voice stopped me.

"Once you return to your platoon, tell Sergeant Johnson I'd like to see him in my office." I nodded and walked to the door, then stopped.

"It won't do any good, sir," I said without turning.

"What won't do any good, Corporal Judah?"

"Johnson will never send me back, so you're wasting our time."

"Why do you think that is, Tom?"

"Because I'm the best man in the platoon and I heard Sergeant Johnson tell you he wanted a whole platoon of men just like me. In this world of war, I survive because I'm the perfect killer, sir."

"There's nothing wrong with wanting to be the best. I think our society pushes that value on us from the time we're born," I heard Jessica say. I shook my head clear of those past thoughts then shivered and looked at her. "What's wrong?"

"Nothing, I was remembering something Dr. Benson once told me."

"Who is Dr. Benson?"

"Dr. Benson and Dr. Feelgood are the same man. Everyone had a combat nickname and his was Dr. Feelgood."

"What was yours," she asked, like this was a guessing game.

"Lazarus."

She looked at me as though the word was foreign to her. "Why Lazarus?"

"Sergeant Johnson said it was because I was baptized in smoke and doom before I was resurrected as a true Prophet from the ashes and sand."

"What were some of the other nicknames?"

"A guy named Danko was called dog."

"Why dog?" Jessica laughed.

"I can't remember," I replied, like I didn't believe my own words.

"Did Sergeant Johnson have a nickname?"

"Yeah… We called him The Goat."

"The goat?" Jessica said, laughing.

"G-O-A-T… It was nothing more than an acronym that stood for the Greatest of all Time."

"Well, I like people who push themselves to be the best. Most people don't have that kind of discipline today." Jessica stopped laughing and smiled.

"Yeah, but people like me take that thought process beyond the extreme."

"So you have a higher work ethic and push yourself harder. There's nothing wrong with that, Tom."

"I pushed myself to the point that I trained my body and mind to become ambidextrous just to give me an advantage no one else had. That is how I work and Dr. Feelgood pretty much said that was wrong in a lot of ways," I explained and slid down and faced her. She gave me a smile that seemed to invite more than I could give.

"Dr. Feelgood was wrong," she said and kissed me. I kissed her back and I let her guide my hand to her breast where I held the bosom of all creation.

I awoke in the pre-dawn hours and eased out of the bed while Jessica slept. I had slept without nightmares and I touched the Native American talisman around my neck, then walked to the window where old routines seemed to linger without consent. I peered outside and scanned the area. Always the same schedule until those engrained habits so become you.

"What time is it?" Jessica asked and yawned.

"About an hour before sunrise," I answered, walking back to the bed without looking at the clock. A cold halo of light seemed to encompass her, green eyes bright and ravenous. She lay there on the bed with her hair splayed about, like a stained sacrifice or perhaps some dark religion born to serve this lesser world of fouler men. I hovered above her as an odd and broken disciple seeking a cure for my wicked hands of time.

Jessica pulled the covers about her and swung her legs over the bed, then ran her fingers through her hair. She had her back to me, her torso draped in a sheet and alight in the pale room like that of a living sculpture conceived in perfect gypsum flesh. "You must have been a runner," I said.

"What makes you say that?" She turned and looked at me over her shoulder like a portrait.

"I can tell by your body type, you're lean so I figured you were a runner at one time."

"I still do."

"Still do... run?"

"Yes, but I'm stronger than I look," she said, letting her hair fall away. She pulled me on top of her naked body, thin arms embracing me like those of a Wiccan performing some ancient rite of exorcism. "An hour before sunrise means we have a couple hours to kill before checkout... and I'm not done with you yet, good sir," she said and kissed me.

Jessica straddled me and took the stone talisman in her teeth like a tainted Delilah, and pulled the jeweled protector until the thin cord broke.

PART 9: Secrets and Lies

A Place of Whispers

"Let the lying lips be put to silence." Psalms 31:18

We checked out of the lodge, then boarded a surrogate bus that grumbled away from the hotel, trailing a sad quaver of dust, leaving behind our peccadillo world of past indiscretions as the squat craft wound through the deserted and scalped mountains like a great phantom bearing a cargo of soiled flesh. Jessica and I made it to the final terminal of our shared journey without further incident, then offloaded the rhombus vessel, holding hands like we were in matrimony among a horde of degenerate clowns. We passed through the Charlestown station, then into the long term parking lot where Jessica's car sat parked like an abandoned child, both dusty and neglected. A cobalt blue GEO Metro—the number one divorced and single economy-cruiser, she told me with a laugh.

We drove through post-industry coal towns where vacant buildings ruled in their ruinous collapse, then peeled the pint-sized vehicle into the southbound flow of interstate 81. Tractor trailers sped by like giant beetles that rattled the car with each sucking draft of air.

"It'll take us about three and a half hours to get home, but I'm going to pull off the interstate in a couple hours to stretch and gas back up." I nodded and stifled a yawned. Jessica noticed and gave me a thin smile. "I take full responsibility for keeping you up all night, so I'll make it up by not smothering you with small talk."

"I don't mind... really."

"No, you can take a nap until we stop for gas. I don't want any excuses later on tonight about you being too tired," she teased. I smiled and rubbed my eyes, then reclined the seat back.

"You don't mind?"

"Nope... I'll even turn the volume down on the radio so it won't bother you," she said and clenched my hand in the way that new lovers do. I started to pull away, but relaxed when I felt the tease of her warm flesh. The soft stroke of her delicate fingers had me feeling too secure. Drowsy and comfortable... the false security of that moment drew me back to a universe of past miseries like a pagan slave to war.

"What's the hardest part for a Marine to accept about killing in combat," I asked Johnson.

"You gotta train your mind to kill without emotion. Most men can't understand that, so they let some kind of moral dilemma trigger their reluctance to fight...that hesitation will always give me an edge, and that's why they call me the Goat...I am the Greatest of all Time."

"How does something like that give you an advantage?" I asked, lighting two cigarettes and handing one over. He took the lit butt and grinned.

"I give myself an advantage by looking at this war from the sand nigger's standpoint," Johnson answered with a shrug, as if his explanation were a well known fact.

"What standpoint is that?"

"If the fucking sand worshippers wanna die for their almighty God and his blessed jihad, then it's my goddamn job to oblige their sorry asses... I do my job without hesitation because I fucking love doing it, and that hunger to be the best at what I do is all the advantage I'll ever need. This war has been a long road and there are many more miles of adversity I have yet to taste, perhaps the end will yet be nothing more than a feast of hardship... but for now, my appetite remains insatiable."

"Just another day in paradise," I heard myself say without thinking. Johnson grinned and stubbed out the cigarette on his palm. He tucked the unfinished stub behind his ear and winked.

"You're learning, Lazarus. You stick with me and I'll turn you into the perfect killer."

I awoke sweaty and saturated from that lingering world of dark prophets and their violent ways, those ghostly faces still echo from my past miseries—and though their voices forever call my name, my heart remains deaf to them all.

"Are you alright?" Jessica asked, looking me over. "You were talking in a weird voice like you were whispering a secret to someone."

"I must have dozed off and had a dream," I said, rubbing my eyes.

"But your eyes were wide open, Tom."

"I know; it's a hard habit to break."

"Sleeping with your eyes open?" she answered, like this was a joke.

"It's a trick you learn when you're in the combat hot zones... it's a habit you never really seem to shake."

"I guess you gotta do a lot of strange things when you're fighting in a war and worrying about what's going on back home," Jessica said and took a deep breath. "Can I ask you a question about the war without pissing you off?"

"Yeah. Go ahead."

"Do you think we need to be over there fighting in Iraq when there's so much wrong with our country right here at home?"

The standard question that seemed to demand a soldier's textbook answer. I thought about what the VA counselors had told me before I replied. "*You have to believe in what you are doing, you have to believe that the greater evil you may commit will override the lesser evils you fight,*" the counselors explained. I believed that lie for so long that once I saw through to the truth of it, it was too late.

"When you are given the belief that you are fighting for a just cause and that motivation will in no way temper your actions, it becomes a very dangerous thing to control, so you don't think about whether the war is right or wrong. You can't think about being politically correct when you're getting shot at, so you look at it from the position that you are the good guy fighting the good fight. You see how lives are changed forever in a combat zone, you witness this on both sides, but it is as simple as fighting for the guy next to you, trying to protect your buddy's life the same way he's fighting to save yours," I told her.

"But we never found any weapons of mass destruction, Tom."

"Every thing over there was a weapon of mass destruction, Jessica."

"So that means you didn't mind fighting in the war?"

"I didn't exactly mean it that way."

"What did you mean?"

"It was an endless mind fuck," I replied. She looked at me, expecting more of an explanation, more details than I wanted to give. I took a deep breath and exhaled slowly. "I guess you could say, when you come back from war, you're left with no spark and you come to realize there is no honesty save that of the innocence you once held. You keep going through the days and nights, trying to find the teenager you were before the war, hoping somehow you'll find the missing virtue you once had, but in all honesty... it feels like your just starting to relive a distant life that was put on pause."

"Well, I saw a spark in your eyes last night, so I think you're fine in that department," she said, pouting her lips in a mock kiss. "Besides, I'm here to take care of you now. After all, we're travel partners." I nodded and felt around my neck for the Indian talisman, but it was gone.

"Do you remembering seeing that stone necklace of mine?" I asked. Jessica glanced my way and gave me a devilish grin.

"The first time we made love, when you were on top, it kept hitting me in the face, almost like the stone was punishing me for being a bad girl. That morning before we made love a second time, I pulled it off with my teeth and you put it on the nightstand. You don't remember that?" I shook my head. "You even said you couldn't forget it because it was blessed or something like that… I'm not sure because we were pretty busy at the time, but you said it in an odd way, sorta like you were gargling mouthwash and talking at the same time."

Jessica parked the car at the gas pump and I got out and stretched as three boys, young men in their late teens, crossed the parking lot. They were thin and owned the asphalt with their enormous, untied brogan boots as big as snow shoes. Random kids from a quiet neighborhood cruising through their day in the way that only a teenager can do during the sluggish summer twilight. The sun was weeping soft leprechaun gold across the broken macadam as it melted into the true face of the equinox, my second favorite time of the day, second only to BMNT when the pre-dawn lust for war is awakened in all soldiers.

There was a restlessness and an urgency about the boys, knowing that soon the sky would draw the drapes on another day, and yet there was also a feeling of fulfillment of what fun or mischief had been accomplished during the past umpteen hours. Tomorrow, another adventure would rise with them as they faced the searing possibilities ahead—I remembered those days and I envied these boys, and yet I pitied them as well, for they wouldn't truly appreciate these times until decades down the road when clocks and schedules and commitments would rule their lost summer leisure.

A kid across the street had the bass amp in his car cranked up to impress a girl with its earth shaking acoustics. His hair was long and he wore those locks with a cool, world-weary outlook on a life that he had yet to experience. Later, he'd talk the girl's parents into letting him take their daughter for a spin in his graduation present and she would be duly impressed and feign fright at the speeds he'd attain. I watched with great interest the ritual between the teenager and his girl: they could become great lovers or remain distant friends, but they would never remember the feeling of being that loose on life, ever again.

I got out of the car as Jessica replaced the pump's nozzle and walked past the young lords of mischief and through the finger stained doors to pay. The woman at the counter was flushed from the steady stream of customers bringing the heat of their seedy day into her air conditioned strip mall world. She wore a host of gaudy bejeweled rings on her fingers, too loose and clunky for her delicate digits as she punched the cash register with her fake press-on claws. The inside of the store exuded a special stench, the mix of cigarettes and sadness and a silent desperation to be anywhere but here. Diet Coke for Jessica and a pack of cigarettes for me; I paid for everything and walked back to the car, looking at the square pack of butts in my hand, and could not explain why I had bought them. I dropped the unopened cigarettes into the trash bin and sat in the car while Jessica went to the restroom. The heat was suffocating, all enveloping. I knew there was somewhere else I had to go, someplace I needed to be in my life… but I could not remember where.

Jessica came back to the car and we were wheeling out of the small lot when she looked over at me and grinned a jester's smile. "I have an idea if you want to hear it."

"Shoot."

"If you're not in a hurry to start school or look for a job right away, my father has a hunting cabin less than a mile from our house. You could stay there for a few days or as long as you like."

"I could use some peace and quiet for a time, but I think you better check with your father before you make that kind of offer to a stranger, Jessica."

She held her cell phone in the air and shook it like an award she had recently won. "I already have and dad said any man that was willing to fight for our country is welcome in his cabin any time. Besides, my dad said he knew some of your family and he doesn't use that old shack for anything except an occasional cook out."

"If you're sure it's alright with your father, it sounds good to me," I answered, looking out the window. The surroundings began to look familiar. "How close are we?"

"We'll be at my house in thirty minutes."

Jessica walked across the shorn yard of stiff summer grass that crunched under her flip flops like broom bristles. Her father got up from his lawn chair and stepped down from the porch, then hugged his only daughter, kissing her head and telling her how much he had missed her, as only a dad can do, until Jessica remembered me and made the introduction. "Tom, this is my father, Clinton Spire." We shook and his hand was hard and callused with the same firm grip as my father's.

"Good to meet you, Tom. Jesse has told me a lot about you and your family. I already know your Uncle Frank. I know your daddy on sight, although I don't think we've ever exchanged a word."

Clinton Spire was tall and long-limbed with a dark square-cut beard that ran to his collarbone. He seemed as if some hermit Hatfield was called back to face a violent thing or perhaps a mountain dwelling McCoy come forth to resurrect an alien feud. "Yeah, Uncle Frank is the more outgoing of the two. Dad's usually pretty shy and quiet until you get to know him," I said.

"My grandfather used to say that a man like your father was just being direct." I looked at him, lost in the meaning until he grinned, his smile like a matted snarl. "I guess it meant your father's the type of man that'll cut through a mile of bullshit and get down to business once his horse is sprung from the chute."

"Yes, sir, that pretty much describes my Dad," I replied and smiled. Clinton Spire rubbed his daughter's back like a charm he'd just found.

"Why don't we jump in my truck and get Tom settled in that ole cabin before it gets too late," he said.

We rode slowly so Jessica could explain the landmarks and tell me how she used to think the cabin was haunted by ghosts as a child. The pea gravel crunched in protest under the tires as the hardwoods along the rutted drive changed to a thicket of yellow pines that seemed to will out all light from the leafless floor below. The cabin sat in a small, hand-chopped clearing, as if it were surrounded by the overbearing arms of a beast.

"There she is," Clinton said, then leaned in and looked across Jessica to where I sat. "Jesse's momma named this patch of ground A Place of Whispers."

"Why?"

"She named it *a place of whispers* because of the way wind whispers through the pine trees," he explained, getting out and walking towards the structure. Jessica opened the door and we stepped inside while her father stood in the cabin's doorway. Clinton Spire thumped the wall of the shack like he was checking the ripeness of a melon. "My wife and I cut and notched every log ourselves and chinked the gaps the same way they did in olden times by using a mix of horse hair and wet china clay that I dug fresh from the South River. Back before the civil war, that clay was prized for its fancy porcelain, but Reuben Judah burnt the South River Clay Company to the ground," he said and paused. Clinton Spire looked at me as if he were now facing some unknown mystery.

I smiled and answered before he could ask. "Reuben Judah was my great grandfather."

"No shit," said Clinton with a genuine grin.

"No shit."

"I heard a lot of stories about that man when I was a young'n; used to scare the bejebers out of me when I was hunting these ridges and hollows alone," he said and seemed to shiver at the memory.

"Every time an owl called or a twig snapped, there was no doubt in my mind it was Reuben Judah coming to scalp me and add my teeth to his necklace. There used to be a poem written about him that went something like…" he started to recite when I cut him off and quoted:

"He owns the night and he rules the day,
His skin is cold to the touch.
He has no blood in earthly veins,
But blood is what he wants.
Scalps of hair and a harvest of teeth,
Jewelry of the mad.
Reuben Judah craves them both,
And your teeth is what he will have."

I finished the poem and Jessica looked at me in a strange way, like she was sniffing out some faint and unseen odor. "I never paid much attention to it, but that stone necklace you lost sorta looked like a black tooth," she said, squinting and surveying my bare neck as if the small relic were somehow still there.

"So Reuben Judah was an honest to God real live person," Clinton Spire interrupted, shaking his shaggy head. I nodded. "So that'd mean all those stories I heard as a young'un wasn't just a bunch of spook stories about the boogeyman."

"No, sir, those stories were real and I've heard them all at one time or another."

"Did they scare you a little?"

"They pretty much had the same effect on me as they did on you," I answered.

"Well, I'll be damned," he laughed. "I want you to come by the house tomorrow evening and we'll pop a few tops and you can tell me a few stories about him."

"Yes, sir, I'd like that."

"Anyway, I better get back to the house," Clinton said and pointed beyond the range of pine trees. "I own this cabin and five acres, but I don't own a damn thing outside this pine thicket. So do me a favor and just don't cross any fences you see, or I'll sure as hell hear about it."

"Alright, let's not get started on that," said Jessica, cutting her eyes.

"There's nothing to start; the Prichard's bought this farm for one reason and one reason only," her father replied with a shrug.

"My ex-husband and his family bought the land around Dad's cabin and posted the property," Jessica explained.

"I've hunted this land since I was a kid and it's not just about them, Jesse. People are flocking to these mountains from up north, buying every acre in sight, and once they get settled in, they treat everyone that's lived in these mountains all their lives like we're some kind of plague."

"It's the same way around Waynesboro. My father looks at them and says that money may be the root of their evil, but envy is still their currency of choice," I broke in.

"Ain't that the truth," Clinton replied as Jessica rolled her eyes. "Jesse can show you around the place and help get you settled in tonight. Just don't forget you owe me a few Reuben Judah stories over a couple of beers tomorrow evening after dinner," he said and started to leave.

"Where do you work," I asked, changing the subject.

"Stuarts Draft Nurseries; do most everything they need at one time or another. I call it a plant, pull, and shoot kinda profession," he said and grinned at his own jape. "I plant trees, pull trees, or shoot varmints and nuisance deer."

"Sounds good to me."

"Well, if you want a job, there's plenty to be had right now," he offered.

"Why?"

"Most of the Mexican workers are sick with some kinda flu, musta brought it up here with them from down south. It ain't even cold weather and they're all sick with the bug," he explained.

"I might take you up on that, I just need maybe a week to rest up from our road trip." Clinton Spire eyed me, thin smile on his lips.

"I could get you hired on as a barnyard pilot, Tom."

"I don't know anything about flying, Mr. Spire." He grinned at me and Jessica.

"You don't need a flying permit to be a barnyard pilot," he explained. I looked at him, not understanding until he started laughing. "A barnyard pilot gets a shovel full of horseshit out of the stall and then piles it outside. That's what a barnyard pile it does, he piles up shit." I dropped my head and laughed.

"Don't feel bad, he tries that joke out on every person who'll listen to him," Jessica explained in my defense.

"Alright then, if you need anything at all, just holler for me up at the house," Clinton said and patted the door frame.

"I'll get Tom unpacked and I'll walk back to the house in a bit," Jessica told her father.

"I reckon, then," he said, still chuckling at his joke and left.

"Let's get started," Jessica said, opening the threadbare cabinets, then waving a hand through the cobwebs and dust motes. "This doesn't look good, so I'll tell you what; I'll fix breakfast at dad's house tomorrow morning and after that, I'll take you into town so we can fill these cabinets."

"That's good with me, Jessica. And thank you… for everything."

"I haven't done anything yet, but I bet you're gonna work up an appetite by tomorrow morning," she answered and gave me a kiss.

Jessica left and I finally took in the interior. The cabin was a single room with a full bed and a hot plate beside the sink holding a lidless, copper pan. The window gave full view of the driveway, and I made a mental note of how far and how much I could see from this vantage point. I did the same routine from every corner and every aspect of the crude shack, both inside and out. It becomes you.

I took one more look around and dropped my pack on the floor, then fell back on the bed and closed my eyes. I was tired. I couldn't remember the last time I wasn't tired and wondered if a man could dry up and die from insomnia. My shoulders ached from the strain placed on the yoked-arm joints. There was no way to avoid the pain. It happens. At least I got to pick when it happened and the amount I endured. I didn't have that option when I slept. I thought about leaving the cabin and going back to the hotel for the necklace the old Indian man had given me, but I twisted my left arm behind my back and drifted off to sleep instead.... My eyes snapped back open, what seemed like only moments later. I was on the floor and it was too quiet; all the night sounds of summer had suddenly vanished to some ancient land of the deaf. I unsleeved my yoked arm and slid across the plank floor then pulled the K-bar knife free of its sheath.

"Tom?" Jessica whispered from the porch. I pushed the knife back into the scabbard and shook out my cramped arm before unlocking and opening the door.

"What are you doing here this late?"

"I thought you might like some company," she said and opened her robe, it slid from her naked shoulders and lay cupped at her feet like a heap of baited desire. She pushed me back inside with her hand and closed the door.

PART Ten: Perfection

Resurrections

"Cry havoc and let slip the dogs of war." William Shakespeare

Our sex that night triggered a craving in me that had once seemed unreachable, something hidden within the cavernous grotto of what I had become. I was no longer sure about anything I was experiencing, and the unspoiled gratification of our lovemaking seemed entirely foreign to me. Maybe it was because I'd suppressed my emotions for three years and I was no longer in control of anything pleasurable I felt, almost as if I unconsciously mistrusted some partitioned and secular part of myself. Jessica's soft cries to my hip-grinding thrusts lingered like unanswered prayers that lay intertwined with the fantasies of a love I had yet to conceive. She fell asleep in my arms and I inhaled deep her sun-scented hair and found it odd that I could now detect *that* fragrance when nothing else would register. Any odor was better than burning rubber or the acidic air surrounding Johnson's cigarettes... anything was better than charred and scalded flesh.

I stared at Jessica's sleeping face. She seemed as though some enchantment were reborn from mythological flesh, cast out from a frozen time to become just another player in my tragic story yet told.

I dozed briefly and awoke to the pain in my cramped and yoked arm with the bed towering over me like a jail cell bunk. I had moved from the cot to the floor again and wondered if I would ever be able to sleep on anything other than the deck with any kind of regularity. There was safety on the floor and there was an unspoken familiarity with the cool ground that all combat veterans understood.

I rose from the floor and shook out the numb arm like a gunslinger, then peeked through the slatted window to take in my conscious world. 0430. The world was asleep and yet I was awake. I knew that somewhere out there, there was someone like me who had snapped awake from their dream reality and was now peering at the nightscape realm of life as I was. Checking the perimeter. Watching for movement. Securing the area while witnessing the violent world and its ways as few others will ever know it. The five minutes I spent at the window was a routine that I was to do for the rest of my days. My odd colored eye was twitching and I felt around my neck for the amulet the old Indian had given me, the absence of that charm had begun to unnerve me in an abnormal way.

"You look good standing there in the moonlight," Jessica said, getting out of bed and dressing.

"Well, you looked pretty damn good lying in bed." She smiled and came over to where I stood and wrapped her thin arms around me; there was too much of her and yet not enough. We stood there looking at each other until she rose up on her toes like a ballerina and kissed me.

"I better get back to the house before dad gets up for work. After all the shit we're going through with my ex-husband, I don't want to worry him."

"I understand," I said and kissed her back, our fat and spicy tongues intertwined like breeding serpents. She pulled away and reminded me with a smile.

"Don't forget, just come on up to the house around 7:30 and I'll make us breakfast. You follow the path we took to get here back to the main road and our driveway is directly across from that."

"I remember, thanks."

"After we eat, I'll take you into town so we can get you some proper groceries and fill up these empty cabinets. After mom died, my dad pretty much lost interest in this place and everything else in his life except for maybe me and his job." I stood, looking down at her like a mute oaf. "You alright?" she asked and cupped my hands in hers. I tightened my grip, then pinned her arms behind her back as if she were under arrest.

"Yeah, I'm fine; better than I've been in a long time." And I was, but only when Jessica was around me and I was conscious to that presence of mind.

"Good," she said, and started to leave when I pulled her back to me.

"Thank you, Jessica." She faced me, tight smile across her lips and dusky eyes alight in the pale glow of an alien moon. Her easy smiles had me feeling secure and protected, and whether or not I deserved such compassion, I could not know.

"I don't think you're the type that says thank you very often, are you?" she replied.

"Not often enough, but I haven't had anything to be thankful for in awhile." Jessica nodded and let her hands slide free of mine, then trotted into the night, flip flops clapping against her feet.

"Don't be late for breakfast and before I forget, there's an old bathtub behind the shower curtain on the back porch if you want to get cleaned up," her voice called back like an unseen wood sprite.

I walked towards the house where Jessica sat on the porch steps with a mongrel hound. The dog dropped to the ground and trotted over to me, wagging his tail. He sniffed my leg and I scratched his head before looking up to where Jessica sat watching. "What's his name?"

She rolled her eyes. "Dad wanted to name him something original so he calls him Buck."

"It looks like he's got a bit of bloodhound in him."

"My father tells everyone Buck's mostly a sooner breed."

"A sooner breed?"

"Yeah, dad says that Buck would sooner shit in the house than shit outside." I laughed and Jessica smiled. "I think that's the first time you have ever honestly laughed around me, it's nice to hear."

Clinton Spire stepped through the screen door stretching, "Morning. Did you get enough sleep last night, Tom?"

"Yes sir... as much as I could."

"Sausage and eggs sound good?" Jessica asked, cutting her eyes at me.

"Anything would be great, thanks."

"Then we better eat while it's hot," she said.

Clinton Spire clapped me on the shoulder as I stepped through the door. "It's gonna be nice to have another man around to talk with for awhile," he said. "Do you fish, Tom?"

"I used to do a lot of trout fishing with my dad before I went into the Marines," I replied, sitting down at the table. Jessica stood at the stove with her back to us, dishing out large portions of scrambled eggs and cakes of crusty and peppered sausage.

"If you follow the fence just outside the front door of my cabin, it'll lead you right to Back Creek, one of the best trout streams in the state."

"I thought you didn't own that."

Jessica sat the food in front of us and Clinton Spire shoved a forkful of eggs into his mouth, then waved his hand as if he were erasing his earlier warning. "No, the Prichard's might own everything inside the fence, but Back Creek and all the mountains around us is part of the George Washington National Forrest and they can't do a damn thing about you, me, or anyone else who wants to do a little fishing."

"After we finish eating, I'm taking Tom into town to pick up a few things," Jessica cut in.

"Pick up some beer and a couple steaks for dinner tonight," Clinton answered and dug out his wallet. I waved off the offer.

"I'll pay for the steaks and beer, Mr. Spire."

"Are you sure? I don't mind at all. And call me Clinton," he answered.

"I don't mind, what type of cut do you want?"

"Always been a t-bone man myself; the honest flavor of beef is hidden in the bone. Tell you what, I got a half dozen old rods and reels in my shed. If you want to do a little fishing, I'll grab you a couple," he offered.

"When I said my dad and I fished for trout, I meant we spear fished."

"Like Indian spear fishing?" I nodded. Jessica stopped eating and listened as I explained.

"My dad's side of the family was mostly Native American, so it's been a tradition for as long as I can remember."

"I almost forgot about you being Reuben Judah's great grandson; he was part Cherokee wasn't he?" asked Clinton.

"He lived with them for a number of years when he was on the run, and he supposedly fathered a bunch of half-breed children from what I remember." Clinton Spire wiped his mouth, set the napkin on his cleaned plate, and got up from the table.

"I'm already looking forward to a good steak, cold beer, and a few Reuben Judah stories. You haven't forgotten have you, Tom?"

"No, sir."

"Fishing with spears; I'd like to try that sometime if you feel up to showing me how to do it."

"I'd like that, Clinton. I'll make three spears so we'll each have our own."

"Was your dad a good spear fisherman?" Jessica asked me. I turned and smiled.

"Yeah, but I was better."

"What made you better?" Clinton asked.

"My dad always beat me at fishing until I was thirteen. After that, my mother would pour water into a wash tub, then drop in ping pong balls. I'd practice spearing the floating balls every day until I could spear ten balls in a row with either hand. After that, my father never beat me at fishing or anything else, ever again."

"Jesus, you weren't kidding," Jessica said like she had finally solved some nameless truth. "You really don't give up when you want to be the best... whether it's against your family or anyone else."

"Not a damn thing wrong with working harder than the next man," Clinton cut in. "I admire a feller that wants to be the best at anything he does, that's nothing but good ole fashioned pride in your work ethics and right there is the main problem with the kids in our society today."

"How's that?" I asked.

"Don't get him started or he'll be late for work," Jessica shoved her dad playfully. He looked down and shook a finger at her.

"I ain't been late nor missed a day's work in twenty-five years, even when your momma was sick. The kids coming up today think their parents owe them something instead of wanting to go out into the world and earn it themselves." I nodded my agreement and his demeanor seemed to ease. "Well, I best get going," he said, looking at his watch and then to his daughter. "Do you need any money for gas, Jessica?" She shook her head.

"No, I'm good." Clinton nodded and said goodbye, then touched a crucifix hanging by the door as he left. I couldn't place it, but there was something wrong about the cross or the prophet nailed to it. Jessica began clearing the table and scraping the leftovers into a pan. "Take the scraps outside and put them in Buck's food bowl while I finish the dishes. After that, we'll head to town and I'll treat you to lunch at the Meadow Muffin."

"Meadow Muffin?" I asked. Jessica started giggling at me like a schoolgirl.

"It's a local burger place where all the rednecks eat their lunch; it's home of the world famous muffin burger and it shocks me to no end that you're almost a local and you haven't heard of it." she teased with her back to me.

The car zipped along the highway that was not unlike the roads I had traveled while growing up—kudzu-smothered banks and the same red clay stains on the asphalt where gully washers swept the earthy taint across the road like a shore now extinct.

Jessica took a right at the first stoplight and pulled into an empty school parking lot. "I got to get some travel vouchers for tomorrow and fill out a bit of paper work. If you don't want to wait for me, you can walk around town for awhile."

"What do you need a travel voucher for?"

"A couple of our teachers have conference in Baltimore for two days; I got volunteered to make the arrangements."

"When are they leaving?"

"Tomorrow morning, but I'm gonna be done with what I have to do around mid afternoon if I can break away from the other women and their gossip," she explained.

"I guess I'll walk around town while you do what you gotta do."

"You want to just meet me at the Meadow Muffin around 1pm? That way we'll miss the usual lunch crowd."

"Yeah, I can do that. Where is it?"

"Once you get into town, just stay on the sidewalk and you can't miss the sign out front. After we eat, we'll get you fixed up with food. Dad also wanted me to ask you if you'd feed Buck for him tomorrow while I'm here getting the women off to their conference."

"I'll make sure he's fed if he'll show me how much to give him and where you keep the food. Is your father going somewhere?"

"Dad's leaving sometime after dinner for a friend's hunting camp to stay the weekend, so you know what that means don't you?" I shook my head. "We'll have the entire place to ourselves tonight." Jessica grinned and met me at the front of her car. "Don't forget, 1pm at the restaurant," she said and gave me a quick kiss, then started off across the lot towards the school.

The sidewalk wound through rows of houses where summer vacation kids had newly awakened to another fine adventure. A boy walked across the road in front of me, flicking his wrist that spat a yo-yo toward the ground, the round sphere zipping along the waxed string like a nether world, spinning along the very cord of its tethered creation...

"How many confirmed kills do you have now, Lazarus?" Johnson asked.

"Two more than you, Sergeant."

"Maybe so, but the day ain't over with yet," Johnson answered and seemed to look beyond the light of our failing day. "Some day, mankind will be subject to a harvest. It will not be one of crops or game; rather, it will be one of death affecting all of humanity. Do you know what that means, Lazarus?" I nodded and started to explain.

"Pretty much; my mother was a certified genius and she had a theory about what you described."

"Enlighten me," Johnson said and grinned.

"Mankind purges every so many thousands of years by regressing backwards, only to eventually progress forward in a relentless pursuit for perfection. Humanity is nothing more than an organism spinning before God from the conception of his creation and ever evolving towards a more advanced existence. The circle's path continues to enlarge as we repeat this process by regressing less each expulsion and

advancing faster until the arc of our evolution orbits the same path forever."

"Just like a yo-yo?" Johnson asked.

"Exactly."

"What is God supposed to be doing while all this is taking place?"

"I asked my mother the same question and she said God was watching us like a child scrutinizes a spinning top. He's sitting there waiting for this grand instrument to stop turning so he can start the wheel of time revolving yet again," I explained and then changed the subject. "Do you know any Bible verses, Sergeant?"

"The only verse I know is one from Revelations...I am the Alpha and the Omega, the first and the last, the beginning and the end."

"Revelations 22:13...It was the first verse my mother had me memorize."

"I like your mother's style, Lazarus."

"So did I."

A horn honked and I blinked back, confused and looking around as if the surroundings were suddenly foreign to me. I looked at my watch, 1:30. A man trudged along the sidewalk on leaden feet, shuffling through the pending heat of the day on old and bent weary legs. "Excuse me, are you from around here?" I asked. He stopped and squinted.

"Why?"

"I got turned around and need some directions."

"I'm not originally from this hillbilly hellhole, moved here from New Jersey last year for my health. Where are you going?" he asked and looked at me, face drawn as if it were an effort for him to exist at all. His hair cropped severe and close like he wore a helmet of grey bristles.

"I'm looking for the Meadow Muffin restaurant," I said.

"You blind or something?"

"What?" I asked. The old man pointed towards the road.

"You're looking at it." I stood there staring at him like a blind man facing the heat of some unknown light source. "It's right there across the street, son. Jesus Christ, what's wrong with you mountain people?" He shook his head and I let him walk away without answering. The old man was angry because the bitterness of his youth now slept in the cradle of mine.

I trotted across the road and into the restaurant that was not unlike most small town eateries. A lone waitress scrubbed a rag across the Formica slab counter, smearing the remnants of other meals and brushing crumbs into the floor, her whitewedge shoes squeaking as she half stepped down the counter on fleshy legs covered in white hose, blue-black webs of varicose veins in hieroglyphic patterns running down her pudgy stovepipe calves.

"Go ahead and grab a seat and I'll be with you directly," she said, waving her dirty rag about.

"I'm supposed to be meeting someone."

"The only people here are a few leftover moochers from the lunch crowd and those three over there," she said tilting her head towards the back booth." They must be having some kinda lover's spat, been arguing and cussing for thirty minutes or more."

I looked towards the commotion and spotted Jessica wedged inside a booth with two men standing over her like carrion seekers. She looked at me as if fear had now crept into the very poverty of her life. I started walking towards the men and Jessica began shaking her head and mouthing the words, *"Please no, Tom."* I stopped at her table and waited with my body rigid and poised for action in the now tacit air.

"Tom, this is my ex-husband, Jim Prichard, and his friend Eddie Marshall." Both men stopped talking and looked at me, sizing me up with their feral eyes.

Jim Prichard had his hair pulled back in a tight ponytail like a male hair stylist. The other man was bald, stubble showing across his dome as if some thin crop were sprouting from his nappy skull. He was the type that shaved his head to prove some manly and boastful point, to show the world he was a bad ass because of his shorn skull without ever having earned the title.

Jim Prichard looked at me, unibrow eyes like they were stitched together with ink. "You know this guy, Jess?"

"We traveled across the country together, he's staying in dad's cabin to fish for a few days," Jessica answered, her voice quiet and eyes averted to the tabletop.

"I guess that means you're fucking him, too," Jim Prichard said, crossing his arms, his bald friend laughed and pointed at me.

"I don't think so, Jim. He's too fucking ugly to screw."

"You two have the etiquette of pigs," I told them.

"You mean I have the manners of an animal?" Jim Prichard uncrossed his arms and grinned at his bald friend like a hooligan.

"I guess that would depend, Jim."

"Depend on what?"

I looked at him and smiled curtly. "Whether or not your mother's a pig fucking whore," I said and stepped face to face with him, a rage from some molten place enveloping me in sinister waves like a pyroclastic flow.

Jim Prichard took a quick step towards me and pushed his now puffed chest into mine; the violation of that contact set all things violent into action. I grabbed his ponytail like a handle and twisted his head left, then brought my rigid forearm across the bridge of his nose. The crunch of bone and cartilage snapped like a frozen twig, my body now moving in perfect combative sync.

His bald friend stumbled toward us on unsure legs and his hesitation proved almost fatal when I shot my right foot out and extended the leg in a vicious kick to his solar plexus; baldy went heels to Heaven over a vacant table like an acrobat. Jim Prichard looked up with weepy eyes, blood and snot on his upper lip like a gruesome slug.

"Knock this shit off and let him up or I swear afore God and all that's holy, I'll bust your head to the fucking white meat," a voice said. I turned and a large black man stood over me with a club made from the sawed off section of a baseball bat. He stood looking down at me like a dark and avenging avatar. "I'm dead fucking serious, boy."

"Tom, please stop," Jessica sobbed from the booth. "He means it, just let it go."

"You damn right I mean it," the black man said and took a step closer. Sirens began wailing in the background, the rage I felt began to pass as I backed away with my hands held clear until my back hit the counter.

PART Eleven: Dr. Feelgood

Dinner of Sorrows

"My feast of joy is but a dish of pain." Chidiock Tichborne

"You wanted to see me, sir?"

Dr. Benson stood up from his desk and gestured toward a vacant chair. "Come in and take a seat, Corporal Judah."

I shrugged and sat down. "What is it this time? Did I squash a bug or do something else that might have offended your professional ethics?"

Benson looked at me and exhaled slowly. "I wanted you to know that I plan on going over Sergeant Johnson's head and start processing your discharged papers, Tom."

"Why?"

"I have conferred with some of my colleagues back in the states and we all agree that you are suffering from a form of fractured identity syndrome brought on by PTSD."

"PTSD?"

"Post Traumatic Stress Disorder."

"You're using that as an excuse to get rid of me, sir." Benson shook his head.

"No... I'm doing this to save your life, Corporal Judah."

"Don't bother doing me any favors, Dr. Feelgood."

"This is exactly what I'm talking about; you don't see it but you are emulating Sergeant Johnson in every way... you want to be just like him."

"No, sir, I want to be better... I want to be perfect."

"Perfect at what, Corporal Judah?" he asked and leaned forward.

"Everything," I said and grinned. "Is that all, sir?"

"For now."

"Am I excused?"

"You're dismissed, Corporal Judah." I snapped to attention and rendered a proper salute, then turned to leave. "Tell Sergeant Johnson I'll be in his office after your platoon has eaten their noon chow."

"I'm talking to you, son," a voice said. I looked through the bars at the uniformed officer as if he were an apparition.

"I didn't hear you," I answered and rubbed my eyes.

"I said my name is Ben Cole and I'm the sheriff of Stuarts Draft. We're going to see the magistrate so move to the back of the holding cell until I get the door open."

I backed away with my hands interlocked over my head. "What am I being charged with?"

The sheriff stepped into the cubicle and pulled out a set of handcuffs. "I need to put these on, so don't give me any trouble, son."

"I don't know what I am being charged with and no one has read me my rights."

"You won't be charged until you see the magistrate," he said, clamping down hard on the metal bracelets until my wrist bones cracked. "Let's go, tough guy," he grinned and pulled me through the door by my manacled hands.

"I didn't start that fight, the other guy did," I tried to explain.

"Yeah, well Jim Prichard and Eddie Marshall tell a different story. I know them and their families, but I don't know jackshit about you." I started to reply when he yanked my hands downward, causing my knees to buckle. "And I really don't want to hear any of your shit so keep your yaptrap shut and do what you're told. You got me?" he asked, bending down and looking me in the face. I nodded mutely.

I was taken to a room where an elderly man sat behind a large oak desk, black robe and white collar like a priest. "You can remove the handcuffs, sheriff," he said. Ben Cole shook his head.

"After what Jim Prichard and Eddie Marshall said about this guy, the cuffs are staying on."

"I honestly don't care what those gentlemen said and this is still my courtroom. Besides, his hands are turning purple and neither Prichard nor Marshall was cuffed when you brought them before my court."

The sheriff spun me around and stuck the metal key in the slot when Jessica opened the door. "May I come in?" she asked. The magistrate motioned her inside with a wave of his hand.

"Are you Thomas Kendall Judah?" the magistrate asked.

"Yes, sir." Jessica looked at me and mouthed the words, "*Are you okay?*" I nodded and she seemed to relax.

"Tom, I put your name in the system and pulled your personal report sheet. Bronze Star, Purple Heart, and a bunch of other medals for bravery while serving in the United States Marine Corps. Is that correct, son?"

"Yes, sir."

"There were a couple of other fights while you were employed as barroom security, but nothing major, so taking into consideration the invaluable service you have rendered this great nation, I find you guilty of disorderly conduct and fine you the sum of 100 dollars. Can you afford to pay the fine at this time, son?"

"Now just wait a goddamn minute, Pete. This guy might be a war hero, but he broke Jim Prichard's nose and cracked two of Eddie Marshall's ribs, and letting him off with a measly—" the sheriff started to object.

"Ben Cole, you might be in the Prichard family pocket, and Theodore Prichard can spend all the cash he wants to get you reelected or get his son out of trouble, but this is still my courtroom and I am still the magistrate for Augusta County. If you question me or my rulings in such a tone ever again, I will find you in contempt and have you arrested by one of your own men. Do you understand me?" the magistrate replied stiffly. The sheriff threw his hands in the air and left.

"Tom, this is Judge David Quillen. His father, Max Quillen, owns the Stuarts Draft Nurseries where my father works," Jessica said.

"Good to meet you, your honor."

He waved a hand as if he were brushing off the introduction. "Just Dave will do, now about paying that fine."

I pulled my belt free and turned it inside out. Inside was a small fold where I kept my travel money and I pulled the bills free. "I haven't seen a real money belt in years," the magistrate said.

"How much cash is that?" Jessica whistled.

"I have a few thousand dollars my mother left me when she passed," I explained and handed over what I owed.

The magistrate smiled and placed the money in his desk drawer, then slammed his gavel down. I flinched. "Case closed," he said and looked at Jessica. "Your motion to have a protective order placed against James Edward Prichard is granted, Ms. Spire."

"Thanks, Dave," Jessica said and started to leave when the magistrate stopped us.

"That protective order states Jim Prichard is to have no direct nor indirect contact with you or your family. Do you understand what that means, Jessica?"

"I think so, but do Jim Prichard and his family understand what it means."

"I'll tell you what it means as far as this court is concerned. Should Mr. Prichard approach you with provocation while you are in the company of Mr. Judah and another fight ensues, there's not a damn thing this court will do if Mr. Judah is forced to defend himself or you should this protective order be violated," he explained.

Jessica wiped her eyes and walked over to the elderly man and kissed the top of his head. "Thank you, Dave."

"You two go on and get out of here before I change my mind," he said, dipping his head and waving us away.

The car backtracked the same rutted and desolate roads, but slower, almost cautious as if Jessica were guiding the vehicle to some faint echo of the past. I wanted to apologize for the fight, trying to find the proper words to right the wrong of my actions.

Jess," I started. She put up a hand and shook her head.

"No, it's my fault. I told the clerk at the school that I was having lunch with you and she must have called Jim when I left."

"Are you sure?"

"No one else knew we were eating lunch at the Meadow Muffin except you and me, Tom."

"Jesus, this town is almost as bad as Waynesboro."

Jessica made a sound like a cough. "I think it's worse."

"Why?"

"In Stuarts Draft, you either work for the Quillen family, planting trees like my father, or you work for the Prichards."

"What do the Prichards do?" I asked.

"They own all the turkey and chicken houses in the area. That's how I got you out of jail so fast."

"How?"

"I called my dad and told him what happened and he told Max Quillen. From there I would say Max called Dave and struck a deal for you."

"I guess your dad is pretty pissed about all of this."

Jessica shook her head and gave a feeble laugh. "As a matter of fact, he said he'd have given a hundred dollar bill to have been there and watch you give Jim Prichard and Eddie Marshall that ass whipping. I'd say everyone in Stuarts Draft knows about the fight by now."

"I guess that's why you're bringing me back to the cabin instead of grocery shopping."

"I'll head back into town and pick up everything for dinner after I drop you off." I didn't like her answer; it bothered me when I knew she was doing it to protect me when I should be protecting her.

"Are your ex and his family that bad?" I asked. She pulled the car to the side of the road and looked at me, eyes weepy and rimmed like the soreness of her heart could be found there.

"I didn't have a choice when I married Jim Prichard. I started dating him when I was a senior in high school even though he was two years older than I was. I guess I was rebelling against my dad and the harder he tried keeping me away from Jim Prichard, the harder I tried to see him. His father had money and Jim already had a job watching over the migrant Mexican workers… And I'll tell you this much, he was as cruel to those Mexicans as he was to me." She wiped her eyes and looked at me, wanting something from me.

"Cruel in what way, Jessica?"

She waved her hand as if to fleece the dead silence of only a moment ago. "Jim knew they needed a job, so he would play cruel jokes on them. He'd make them think they were fired for no apparent reason or the immigration department was going to deport them, and once they started crying, he'd call his buddies in the office and laugh at them. Sometimes he would dock them an hour's pay if one of the Mexicans got mad at his jokes."

"And you?"

"And me what, Tom?"

"If he was the same way with you… why did you marry him?"

"He got me pregnant." I looked at Jessica and she folded her arms across the steering wheel and buried her face without looking at me. "I didn't get pregnant like that. A couple of his friends and his brother Bennie held me down one night after our high school football game while Jim raped me. Jim and his father wanted me to get an abortion when they found out I was pregnant, even offered to pay for it… but I couldn't stand the thought of doing that."

"So you got married instead." She nodded.

"It wasn't so bad at first. His father gave us a house to live in and I was going to school to earn my teaching degree. But Jim began to fail at things and then he would drink and take it out on me. He knocked me down and kicked me one night while I was in my second trimester and I lost my babies."

"Babies?"

Jessica tilted her head back and sighed, then looked at me. "I would have had twin boys, but he pretty much killed them. The doctor said most abnormal pregnancies are aborted in the first or second trimester, but I would still be able to have other children. I never told the doctor about Jim kicking me, nor did I tell my father."

"Who else knows?"

"Only you," she said, starting the car and pulling back onto the road.

"Why did you tell me, Jessica?"

"I dunno... maybe it's because I can trust you, or maybe it's because you stood up for me when you didn't have to," she explained, pulling up to the cabin. "I'll run back to town and meet you at our house around six if that's good with you."

"Yeah, that'll be good."

"Don't be late this time," she forced a smile and wiped her yes. "Besides, I have a surprise for you after we eat and my dad leaves."

I walked towards the porch where Clinton Spire stood watching three steaks on a cheap Wal-Mart grill, beer in one hand and a set of grilling tongs in the other. "Already two ahead of you," he said, tilting a beer in my direction. "Go ahead and grab yourself one out of the cooler just inside the door."

I took a can and popped the top. "Clinton, I want to," I started apologizing. He shook the tongs in my direction and took a sip of his beer, then swallowed.

"I don't want to hear a damn thing about you being sorry, Tom. I'd have given my left nut on a chopping block to have been there and watch you break that sonofabitch's nose."

"Alright, dad… don't get started," Jessica yelled through the door.

"This makes you somewhat of a local hero. And you busted some of Eddie Marshall's ribs is what I've been hearing around town," Clinton added in a lower voice.

"That's what the sheriff told the magistrate," I said and took a seat in a ratty and faded lawn chair.

"You were just lucky the other'n wasn't there, that crazy fucker is the worst one of the bunch."

"Which one?"

"Jim Prichard's younger brother, Bennie. He's the one everybody calls Mr. Bojangles."

"Why in the hell do they call him Mr. Bojangles?" I asked.

"Because he's fucking retarded," Clinton started chuckling. "One minite, he'll be standing there pretty as you please and the next second, the crazy bastard will start dancing for no damned reason."

"He's not retarded," Jessica said, backing through the door, plates rattling in her arms.

"That little asshole is nuttier than a pile of squirrel shit," Clinton answered over his shoulder.

"He's not retarded; Bennie has Asperger Syndrome... and nobody calls him Mr. Bojangles to his face," Jessica explained to me.

"Why not?"

"He's a crazy sonofabitch, that's why," Clinton cut in.

"Just because his Asperger syndrome makes him do abnormal things from time to time, it doesn't mean he's crazy or retarded."

"Steaks smell good," I said, changing the subject.

"Yup, and ready for the plate," Clinton said, taking the meat off the grill and stacking them on a dish. "How much longer before the bean casserole is ready, Jesse?"

"Fifteen minutes," she said, wrapping the plates of grilled meat in tin foil and disappearing back inside.

"That oughta give us enough time to talk about your great granddaddy," said Clinton.

"Alright, I'll tell you as much as I know."

"Why did he kill all those people and burn their houses down?'

I finished my beer and opened another can before I spoke. "Reuben Judah never liked slavery, but he was like Robert E. Lee and torn between what he believed in and his home, so he did the same thing as Lee and stayed with the state of Virginia when the Civil War broke out. He was an oddly devout man, but a man of considerable means— owned land and live stock, preacher at the local church he founded— but he was always drawn to the woods and mountains."

"Why?" Clinton cut in. I took a sip of beer and swallowed.

"He needed to be in those mountains so he could work things out in his head is what my dad would say when I asked that question. It was his knowledge of the mountains and his survival skills that got him assigned to John Singleton Mosby as an assassin."

"I bet he was damn good at that job," said Clinton. I nodded.

"Probably too good. It caught Sheridan's eye and he marched into the Shenandoah Valley looking for Mosby and Reuben Judah. When he couldn't find John Mosby or his men, he started burning everything in the valley to the ground. A few of the politically connected families around Waynesboro contacted Sheridan's command and had their farms spared because they told him what they knew about Reuben Judah and showed the Union Army where his family lived."

"Damned if I ever knew about that. What happened?" Clinton asked.

"Most of Reuben's family was hung and his house and crops were burnt. His two sons, Eli and Luther, escaped to Atlanta and raised their families, and then moved back to Waynesboro after the war ended. Once Reuben found out his family was murdered, he was given a discharge by Mosby... I guess the rest of what went on with Reuben Judah is what's become his legend."

"Let's eat," Jessica yelled.

"We better grab it while it's hot," Clinton said, closing the lid on the grill. "I guess having your family killed like that would make most any man go a little crazy."

"Yes sir... but Reuben Judah wasn't just any man," I answered.

I opened my eyes with a strange hand hanging in my face like a cadaver. I adjusted my eyes and realized I was on the cabin floor and Jessica was still in bed. I slid out from under her fingers and walked to the window.

"What time is it?" Jessica asked and yawned.

"0430," I said without looking. I knew.

She looked at the jagged purple welts carving a path across my leg. "Did you get those in the war?" I nodded.

"Yeah, the hummer I was riding in hit an IED. That's why Johnson gave me the combat name, Lazarus."

"Because your vehicle hit a bomb?" I shook my head.

"I used to wear a brown contact lens to cover my odd eye so it would make me look normal. When our hummer hit that IED, it blew the iPod out of my ears and knocked my contact lens out. After I recovered and got sent back to my unit, Johnson and everyone else thought my eye changed because of the blast I took to the head."

"You didn't tell them anything different?"

"There wasn't any sense in trying. I couldn't get another contact lens to cover my eye, so I left it the way it was." Jessica nodded and stretched, then slipped out of bed.

"I gotta meet the other women at the school in an hour to issue their travel vouchers and finish the paperwork for their trip, which reminds me," she said, starting to dress. "I'll probably stay in town awhile so I can pick up a few things for us."

"Why?" I asked.

"I'm taking you to a special place for a little camping trip. I got you stocked up here, but if you get bored, there's a key under the milk can on our porch if you want to stay at the house after you feed Buck. You can watch TV if you want."

"Never watched it much, Jessica."

"We've got cable."

"I grew up without a TV in my house."

"Jesus, why?"

"My mother started homeschooling me and she thought it would become a distraction," I explained, pulling on my jeans.

"I couldn't have lived without TV when I was in high school."

"I didn't have a choice, but it paid off in the end."

"How?" she asked, scratching her nose.

"I took the SAT's when I would have been a high school junior and earned the third highest score."

"In the state?"

"No," I said and smiled. "In the entire country for both juniors and seniors."

"I bet your mom was grinning from ear to ear."

"Not really," I said, tucking my shirt in.

"Why wasn't she?" Jessica asked, smoothing down her hair.

"Because two other people had better scores than I did. Even though, because of my test score I was classified as a genius, it wasn't good enough for her."

"Why?"

"Because I would never be classified as a true genius like she was." I shrugged as if the achievement no longer mattered.

"A genius is a genius… and I think that's impressive as hell for you to accomplish."

"Thank you, but there's a difference, Jessica."

"What kind?"

"I can control what I do and fully understand the process in which I achieve my goals; a true genius only understands that he or she can do a certain task without understanding the process by which they do it. And most true geniuses are similar to my mother, meaning they cannot understand why everyone can't be as perfect as they are," I explained, feeling for the necklace.

"Where's your necklace, Tom?"

"It's at that West Virginia hotel we stayed in."

"I gave your necklace back to you last night, that was part of the surprise I told you about and taking you camping to get us out of this town until the rumors die down was the other part. I called the hotel and they still had your necklace in their lost and found, so I paid to have it sent here overnight… You don't remember?"

"Yeah, I remember now," I lied.

"What did you say, Tom? You mumbled something."

"I was just thinking out loud. So you'll be back sometime this evening?"

"Yeah, give or take an hour or so," she smiled and elbowed me. "I'll bring you something good."

"I wish you didn't have to go," I said before I could stop the words from spilling out.

"I know," Jessica replied and hugged me. "But I won't be too long. Besides, it's only for half a day or so."

"I know… I'll be fine."

"Dad left some poles in the shed if you decide to go fishing," Jessica said, breaking away and grabbing her keys.

"I might do that, thanks." She walked back over to where I stood and pulled me to the porch then gave me a kiss.

"Are you gonna miss me?" she asked, straightening my collar like a proper housewife.

"More than you probably know," I said and smiled. Jessica blew me a kiss and then dropped off the porch. I watched the fading red glare of her taillights until they snuffed out to blackness. And the loneliness of my world joined with that emptiness and there was no escape from that union.

PART Twelve: Death Before Dishonor

A Wicked Game

"It's strange what desire will make foolish people do,"

Chris Isaak

I must have dozed off and awoke on the porch as the first specters of life began stirring among the pre-dawn shadows, infant flickers of movement as if the phantoms of creation itself were now being reborn from a dead and forgotten time. Small birds skipped along branches, ducking their ever-watchful heads as they searched the lingering nightscape for predators; a raccoon moved, hunched and silent among the pines, scrounging a last minute meal like a bandit set loose from an outlaw clan. I felt around my neck again for the ancient amulet and its absence unnerved me. The Native American necklace was like so many in my life that sent me chasing after some revelation hidden in a maze that no longer leads me anywhere. It becomes an all encompassing sand trap like the canary's last song in a dark and belligerent mine, sad bird eyes watching as the candle's flame begins to slowly wink out. You find yourself wondering what really lurks behind the closed doors of your shallow and forgotten world. And it's all about that attention… or lack thereof. It's about asking every question to right the wrongs, but never receiving the solution. It's about having to feel for the very fabric of a life you no longer wear or control… and everything around you requires an innate sense of perfection which you no longer seem to possess..

I felt like I was losing touch with the moral compass guiding me, spinning out of control like a comet dropping from the constellations of pain into an endless metaphysical void. I looked toward the cracked sky and could not remember ever feeling this strange. It felt like I didn't know who I was anymore, like I was some odd form of antisocial pollen that spread upon the reeking and war torn winds of deceit. I realized then that I was close to the abyss Dr. Benson had spoke of, its dark reach all encompassing and beyond the measurements of mortal men.

I walked to the Spire house and fed their dog and then followed the fence line to the fishing spot at the base of the mountains Clinton Spire had mentioned. The creek was as wide as most rivers and I let the sound and the fury of crackling water guide me along the aggregate shore. I found myself thinking about home and those few friends that now seemed hard years and long miles away. They had meant well, but it was always their probing questions, asking what it was like to kill another human being so they could live out that rush vicariously through me.

When you're asked what war is like by those well-meaning friends or family, you never tell the truth. You can never relate to them the real stories they want to hear, those tales that drive some insatiable lust in them to actually feel—through your words—the dark deeds of death. But the real truth is you don't want to remember, so you partition that part of war out, you find yourself replacing it with other memories to override those nightmares. I never stared too long at the horrible wounds or the grimace of death stitched across those young faces.

I looked at their hands instead, hands that were blunt and dirty from hard labor, hands that were sometimes clean and thin and delicate— feminine fingers that belonged on the neck of a violin or a cello in some disturbing symphony. Instead, those hands had wired bombs or pulled the triggers of rifles, hands that once fired RPG's or threw rocks until we turned those fingers into cold claws of death... Only when those hands ceased to move did we feel safe again.

No one wants to hear about the hands because the real side of war you experience has neither the memory nor that burden of guilt.

I got back to the cabin and found Jessica waiting on the porch, clutching her knees, head buried into her folded arms. "What's wrong, Jess?' She waved off my comment with a toss of her hand.

"Nothing, Tom." I suddenly remembered what Jessica had told me about Jim Prichard's rape and pictured her ex-husband and his brother sliding their hands up her shirt, groping her breasts crudely in some dark and tucked away place while the alien hands of his friends held her down. I could see them laughing and feeling her up while she cried out at their cruelty, pleading for them to stop their spectacle of sorrows.

"Something's gotta be wrong. Was it your ex-husband again?" She looked up, eyes red-rimmed with regret.

"Living in a small town where everyone knows everyone's business is what's wrong. When I got to the school, the whole faculty treated me like I was some kind of a cheap whore."

"Why?" She looked at me and shrugged mutely instead of answering. "It's because of me and the fight I got in with Jim Prichard isn't it?" Again, Jessica waved off my question with a flip of her hand, then rested her chin on her arms and looked towards the mountains.

"Do you ever wish you could just give up on this whole fucking rat-race thing and rejoin the human race?" I sat down beside her, feeling the pains of guilt because of her grief. Jessica sighed then continued.

"Why do we have to set ourselves apart and pledge allegiance to schools and bratty children who didn't even ask to be born? Why do we have to constantly raise our freak flag, or put an apple on our desk as a symbol for people to see that we're one of the good guys?"

"It's your way of making the world a better place one day at a time, Jessica."

"Did you make the world a safer and better place when you were in Iraq, Tom?"

"I'd like to think I did, but I didn't have much choice then." She nodded and our eyes met.

"So what does it matter if our life ends up looking like something else? Have you ever thought that maybe we're just the perfect metaphor for being losers, or the perfect simile for being shitheads, or nothing but muddy door mats to everyone and everything around us? Would any of this really matter even if we could turn our world on to a brighter place with the flick of a switch? Or would it be better if we crossed Narcissus with Icarus and watched everything and everyone around us burn to ashes?"

"Even the Phoenix went through the tribulation of fire to arise from the ashes stronger and more beautiful, Jessica. I've went through my fire and I'm still going through the burnt cinders of my transformation. Divorce is a pain in the ass and you're just getting started on yours, but it gets better."

"Promise?"

"You'll begin to make progress a little bit at a time," I said. She wiped her eyes and smiled.

"Sometimes it looks like progress, it feels and smells like progress, and yet there are the smallest egg shell fragments of my life spread out on the pavement for the world to finish crushing. Sometimes it feels like I am ricocheting off the sides of my own life. I used to have a set of beliefs, but I don't believe in them anymore." Jessica leaned close and gave me a hug. "Thank you for listening, Tom."

"You're welcome, and you're not alone, Jessica. I went through… or rather, I am still going through the same changes in my life. Sometimes I feel like I am Houdini and I can't escape the perfect chains of destiny I have created for myself. I see and feel the scars that I have, but no one else can see them nor understand the ugliness of what they represent."

"I don't think scars are ugly at all, Tom."

"Really?"

"A broken heart leaves a scar no one can see, but once you learn to love again, it heals over and makes the heart stronger."

"Yeah, I guess you're right," I said and hugged her closer. "You should quit teaching and start working with veterans in the VA hospitals." She smiled back and kissed me lightly on the cheek.

"I might just do that one day. Now let's get dad's truck loaded up and head out of here. I'd like to have our camp set up before it gets too dark on us."

"Where are we going?"

Jessica pulled away and grinned. "I thought we'd head up to the Bee rocks."

"B rocks?" She shook her head.

"Not B... it's Bee," she corrected and made a buzzing noise. "Like honey bees."

"How did a set of rocks get a name like that?"

"When the first settlers crossed over the mountains and made their homes in the Shenandoah Valley, they found a large outcropping of stone near the top of Bald Mountain. They would place bowls of sugar water on the rocks as the sun was setting, and when the bees came to drink, they'd douse them with flour."

"Flour?"

"Yeah, that way the bees would be solid white and the spotters could follow their path of flight, using the rocks as a lookout point and call out directions to the chasers until they found the hive. After that, they'd wait until morning when the dew was thick and smoke the bees out of the nest and harvest the honey."

"No shit," I laughed.

"No shit, and that's how the Bee Rocks got its name. It'll take an hour to get to the top of the mountain in dad's truck and then we'll have to walk a bit."

"Walk. How far, Jess?"

"Only about a hundred yards or so, but I'll have to lead the way."

"Why?"

"If you don't know where you're going, you can walk right off the edge of the rocks instead of going through the middle of a laurel thicket until you come out on a wide plateau."

"How far would you drop if you fell off?" Jessica looked at me and made a whistling sound and moved her hand in a downward half-arc like a diver.

"About a couple hundred feet to the boulders below, at least two or three drunks go over the edge every year because the local kids like to party up there at night. When me and my friends partied on the rocks, we would wear cow bells around our neck so everyone knew where we were and how to find anyone if they got lost."

"Jesus, where are you taking me?"

"It's one of the most beautiful unknown places in the Blue Ridge Mountains," she said and nodded towards the truck. "If my big tough Marine is done with being scared, I'm ready to head out." I laughed at her comment and got in the passenger seat.

Jessica sawed the truck's wheel and pulled to the curb of a road-side store. "I want to grab a couple six packs and stick them in the cooler," she explained. "You need anything while I'm in there?"

"No, I'm good," I answered and stretched while looking over the gravel lot and the gathered collection of local humanity.

A woman next to the truck just finished using a crusty rag to wipe the nose of her child while changing its soiled diaper on the floor of her minivan. She held the putrid remnant at an arm's length and carried it to the trash receptacle as if it were some reeking effigy sent forth from one Hell to calm another, or perhaps a prize shared by the single self-loathing mommies every where. Dirty diapers and dish pan hands and a silent desperation to be anywhere in their raw and blistered redneck lives but here, never realizing they are just one Wal-Mart refill away from another hopeless and invalidated addiction. She whipped her hair into a tight ponytail, then walked back to her vehicle like some fallen and wasted suzerain or perhaps a tainted Medusa, her bitter steps clopping a sad pittance that hid any real beauty behind the mommy mask she wore before her world.

At an outside picnic table, a woman in her seventies or so had Parkinson's. Her hands and body were shaking uncontrollably, one hand clutched and clawed and useless in her lap from an earlier stroke —it was painful to watch. The man beside her held a bottle of juice to her mouth and she took a shallow sip through a straw. I could read his lips… "More?"

Yes, she shook out the answer with a palsied nod of her cronish head and again he lifted the straw to her mouth. When she was finished, he held her icy and emotionless hand and for a time, the shaking eased until it started up again and their hands shook together as one. The scent of her perfume wafted to where I was sitting, a jaded and reeking essence I could not quite put my finger on... that subtle fragrance of the dying.

Did it matter what I was thinking? How many times the same elderly couple had sat at that table alone and unnoticed? Like them, each of us would struggle both muted and oafish against our own private and colliding worlds, letting the train of fate carry us into our rural towns and our big cities, into regret-filled nights, into our tumble of unmade beds and our forgotten sleep. The lights of our lives were all on, the clockless world was ablaze with those unknown possibilities and the distant dreams that remain boundless and yet fulfilled.

I closed my eyes and tried to imagine them young, on their honeymoon, or on a train to a weekend getaway in New York or Philadelphia. He lit her cigarette and she took a long, satisfied pull. She stepped down from the train and walked ahead of him in her clunky shoes. He stopped to admire her small breasts and the way her hips stirred that red skirt, a cold halo of light seeming to encompass her, green eyes bright and ravenous. She stood rooted to the world as the sun caught her hair like a stained sacrifice or perhaps some holy avatar born to rule this lesser world of fouler men.

Hey baby, we're gonna live forever, he yelled to her. She turned and winked over her shoulder like a living sculpture, already smitten and intoxicated with the power she held over him.

She fell in love with him when they first danced. Her wearing those cold flapper shoes and he dressed ever so dapper and dark. It began with a bow, a practiced dip and then a shy kiss of perfection. It was lightening trapped in time—a single and fleeting radiance that should have lasted forever—now he was a soul mate to the aged and soulless, for better or for worse, in sickness and in health and he was solitary to the inspiration that those who walked past them might take their sad tale and make it better.

It's hard to know what is true and righteous in this world. Hard to know if the fading and glowing sun is nothing more than a gateway to an alien world we have yet to explore. Hadn't I come here to be persuaded? Hadn't I come to steal and plunder and laugh at my hubristic mortality like a berserker chasing down some ancient pagan prophesy?

I sat in the truck, but my mind kept racing back to a scene in which the old man was young and standing guard like a depraved vendor before a broken and barren crib. I kept going back to a scene where the old woman was young and locked inside a deserted gas station rest room, kneeling in judgment before a frozen and unvoiced God.

The bats were out and they stained the sky as they skirred the humid air for a mothy meal in the pale and forlorn evening. I got out of the truck as Jessica exited the store, one of the gristly-winged bats dipped down from the Heavens toward her. I grabbed Jessica as she swatted the air and swept her up in my protective arms. We laughed and spun in a circle beneath the soft lamplight like an obscene ferriswheel conceived in flesh. The elderly woman and the man stood side by side at the picnic table, her ancient soul bared and suffering like a strangling sparrow, his arm around her shoulder like tarnished refugees as they watched with great sad eyes our young dance unfolding before them.

Every day the woman would stand gnomish and shaking by the same table, watching the spot where mine and Jessica's first dance took place and perhaps pondering the anti-blessings of that arousal. Would she remember how we twirled and laughed beneath the bats? Would she close her eyes and stop shaking for a brief flitter of time before the tremors begin again in that jerky and rhythmic dance?

Through her window of yesteryear, there was only that dim tabernacle of time... already lived and so long ago, but yet it seems to her as if it all happened only yesterday. Is that what the woman's rheumy eyes behold when they were closed and she looked back through the acoustic shadows of her own life? Did she measure her remaining time in days or kisses? Did her eyes beg to see something different while she fought against that slow ascension of stairs to some fat and gilded Heaven just beyond her reach?

"What's wrong?' Jessica asked as we pulled away. I nodded my head towards the couple.

"Do you know them?"

She looked over her shoulder to where the elderly couple stood watching. "Nope... why?"

"No reason," I replied.

Jessica wheeled out of the parking lot and I turned to watch the man and woman turn to a soft grayish color and then fade into nothingness. I was more afraid of growing old, waiting for the tides of age to clutch me with feebleness, scared of facing that fate alone. I kept my eyes on the elderly couple until I could see them no more and realized then that I would never know their names... and it did not matter.

PART Thirteen: The Bee Rocks

Perfection

"This is the very perfection of a man, to find out his own imperfections." Saint Augustine

We jostled about in the cab as Jessica negotiated the 4-wheel drive through a series of switchback roads that were no more than old rut washed fire breaks. The steep slopes gave way to deep gorges where lone pine trees sat ravaged and limbless like some horrible fire had sought them out, their stark existence nothing more than dark splinters jutting from the land and all were reduced to nothingness from the misguided bands of gypsy moths or other winged parasites of their kind.

We ceased to talk and let the beauty of those distant wilds speak of its immaculate conception—the hidden and unknown grottos far beneath the truck seemed to suck through the vehicle and pull the marrow of what we were into the core of it, into the hidden histories of the mountains and those unsung ballads of a star-crossed love yet woven upon their seasonal winds.

Jessica downshifted and sawed the wheel. "I can tell my really dad likes you, Tom."

"Really?"

"I think it's because you're both so much alike."

"Such as?"

"When you were telling us at breakfast how hard you work to be good at everything you do, it touched a nerve in him. My dad is always telling me, 'Trust that you have the capability to harness and possess the greatness inside of you.'"

"And you don't believe that, Jess?"

"Oh I believe it, but sometimes greatness doesn't seem to surface for me no matter how hard I try."

"Then you gotta push those failures away and work harder until you achieve your goal... it's always worked for me," I said to boost her lack of confidence.

"That sounds like something my dad would say," she chuckled and then took on a more serious tone. "You see, to everyone in Stuarts Draft, my father is only a tree planter, but if you ask him, he'll tell you that the saplings he puts in the ground sing to him. When I tell dad everyone else thinks they're nothing but trees, he says he doesn't worry about that aspect of it because he's never once set out to plant a great tree, just harvest one that's useful or beautiful to anyone who cares about such things. He said to trust that there's something inside you, something simultaneously human and ultimately divine, something that will come out in the work you do to make the finished product of your efforts shine. And you're just like him, Tom. You both keep pushing yourselves until your efforts shine in some perfect way."

"Yeah, I guess that pretty much describes us."

"And it's not a bad way to be," Jessica added and stopped the truck where the road came to an end between two faded stumps. "This is as far as we can drive, so we'll have to load the camping gear into our backpacks and walk the rest of the way."

We got out and hitched up our packs like day tripping hikers and started walking downward to a point that seemed to fall off the known world and into a wall of high-banked laurel, Jessica leading the way while tapping a bent ski pole to test the ground as she walked.

"You can't see the cliff from this mountain laurel, but the foot path we're on is only about three feet wide, so walk exactly where I walk."

"Gotcha."

We broke through the jungle-thick bracken and walked out onto a smooth limestone plateau that ran a few hundred feet in each direction. The end of the large jutting rock gave a panoramic view of the immense mountains in all directions, as if the world itself was shorn up from the unknown depths below and we now stood on a pedestal to witness this silent creation. I walked and inspected the graffiti that adorned the stony surface as Jessica stood back and smiled. "You see... I told you it was beautiful."

I knelt and let my fingers trace the chiseled names and faded dates of people long dead that were etched by hammer and iron into the green-blue surface, granite effigies from the back chambers of some unknown cathedral of time. Jessica walked up beside me and touched my shoulder. "Go over to the edge, it'll give you the best view of all," she whispered as if her voice might taint these ghostly saints of mountain lore.

I let her lead me to the end of the outcropping where the long valley stretched out below like and ancient chaparral, green and verdant with clouds edged of orange brawling in the high and brutish winds as they crept across the pastoral sky.

"God Almighty… this is as close to perfection as you can get," I heard myself say. Jessica hugged me close and kissed my cheek.

"I'm glad you like it. I knew you would," she said and pointed at a small brown dot below. "That's my dad's cabin and believe it or not, you could walk to the front door from here quicker than you could drive to it. And right below these rocks is where the natural spring that feeds Back Creek starts, so I was sorta thinking," Jessica said with a wry smile.

"About what?"

"We've got two choices for dinner," she answered, surveying the pending campsite. "I can roast us some hot dogs over the fire, or you can show me how good your fishing skills really are and spear us some fresh brook trout."

I looked at Jessica and grinned, then slipped the K-bar knife free of its sheath. I took a waterproof bag out of my rucksack and started towards the thicket to cut a pole for a spear.

"Three fat trout sound good enough?" I asked over my shoulder.

"I'll believe it when I see it," she chided and shooed me away with a toss of her hand. "You go get 'em, tiger. While you're gone, I'll get everything set up and our gear stowed away."

I cut a hickory stave and began shaving it down as I dropped off the slope to the sound of water pattering against the stones. Along the rugged terrain, sprigs of wild asparagus grew in lime green stalks like the medicinal stems of some defunct fairy world. I gathered enough of the thick-coned tips for our dinner, then slipped along the stream's course until I found a deep, slow moving pool. I moved a few yards further downstream, then eased my bare feet into the spring current, being careful not to disturb the rocks, keeping my shadow from the water's surface while watching upstream towards the eddy where the torpedo-bodied trout wimpled in the velvet current. Their waiflike fins fanning as the inside of their gill plates grew red-rich with blood, across their mossy green backs, a loom of black lines woven into a pattern like some faint language from a forgotten time. I was in my element and let the whispered memories from my past guide the spear tip towards the band of renegade trout. "*Always keep your tip just under the water and to the left of your target, that way when they bolt towards cover as your spear's shadow crosses over them—they will swim into the prongs of your spear.*" My father had taught me that and I let those long ago lessons prove worthy until I had three trout in my waterproof bag soaking the pre-gathered asparagus.

Jessica sautéed the asparagus in butter and then pan roasted the trout in the same cast iron skillet over the open flames of our fire. The rib cradle of our dinner lay bare on the rocky surface as if some long extinct fossil had now been pulled back from the stones of its prehistoric tomb.

"Damn that was good. The fish had an asparagus flavor that seemed to seep through the butter and into the meat," I said.

"It was good and I usually don't eat asparagus," Jessica replied, rolling the leftover fish bones into a rack of tin foil.

"You don't like asparagus, Jess?"

"It makes my pee stink," she replied and laughed at her personal observation.

"It's because of methyl mercaptan."

"Methyl what?" Jessica asked, wiping her hands with a sanitary wipe then handing me one from the container.

"Methyl mercaptan; it's a type of sulfur-containing compound that's found in eggs, feces, and skunk urine."

"And that's what makes my pee stink?"

"Yup. But not everyone has that problem, some people have a built in immunity to the side effects of methyl mercaptan...like me."

"Jesus, how did you know that, Tom?"

"I guess growing up without a TV gave me more time to read, so I read anything and everything I could get my hands on. My Uncle Frank used to call me the encyclopedia."

"I believe it, my dad even made a remark that he could tell you were smart. Or as he put it, sharper than a rat turd on both ends." We both laughed and then sat watching the fire, the small flames now reduced to a flicker above a bed of molten coals. "After you left the other night, he told me the story of Reuben Judah."

I nodded without taking my eyes off the fire. "He was quite a man."

"You can't blame your great grandfather for what he did, especially after most of his family was killed and his house burned to the ground."

"What he did during the Civil War was one thing, but he killed people for revenge and that made him a murderer, Jessica."

"I would think it's unfair to judge your great grandfather that way."

I stirred the coals to life with a stick, then spoke softly over a glitter of orange motes winking out above our heads. "Exodus 20:1, Thou shalt not murder."

"I can buy that, but even God murdered when he caused the great flood, Tom."

"God did not murder, Jessica. He killed in order to preserve the last fragment of beauty, to save the last grain of perfection that lived in his grandest creation. That was why Noah and his family and all of the animals were spared. Do you honestly want to know the truth about Reuben Judah?" Jessica looked at me, but said nothing, eyes replacing her words as though she were a confessor looking deep into the scarred and abraded soul of a sinner. "Do you really want to hear what my family has kept hidden and secret from the rest of the world for more years than I care to count?"

"If this is upsetting you, we can change the subject and talk about something else, Tom."

"To be honest, I don't mind talking about what Reuben Judah was. It's being compared to him because we have the same last name is what bothers me the most. When people in my hometown found out I had just returned from Iraq, they seemed to think I would start scalping people and pulling their teeth."

"I don't see that happening." Jessica smiled and my temper subsided. She opened two cans of beer from the cooler and handed me one.

"When my dad was a boy, a man came to visit his family's house. This man was a reporter from San Francisco and he wanted their permission to publish a book about Reuben Judah."

"How did the story of your great grandfather travel all the way to the west coast?"

"It didn't actually. The man heard the story directly from Reuben Judah himself." Jessica looked at me, not understanding what I had just told her. "Reuben Judah was confined to a San Francisco mental institution under the name Luther Eli Cobb."

"How long ago was this, Tom?"

"The mid-1950's; my dad was just a kid at the time."

"I don't see how that would be possible, that would make your great grandfather over—"

"He was 118 years old," I said, cutting her off. She shook her head in disbelief.

"That's impossible... Did your family believe the reporter?"

"Not at first, but he told us things about Reuben that only our family knew."

"Like what?"

"His first and middle names for one, Luther and Eli were the names of his sons."

"And his assumed last name?"

"Cobb?"

"Yeah," Jessica replied, tucking her legs and leaning forward.

"Reuben Judah was known throughout the mountains as the Prophet of Cobb Hollow."

"But those things could be nothing more than a series of coincidences, Tom"

"But there was one distinct trait that wasn't a coincidence. Eli Cobb had one brown eye and one blue eye." I looked away from the fire and into the veil of darkness around us.

"There's something else, isn't there?" Jessica asked.

"There were the scars Reuben Judah had that only my family knew about, but never told another living soul."

"What kind of scars?"

I sighed and explained. "Crosses." Jessica said nothing and waited, enraptured with the story like a child hearing a ghostly tale. "When Reuben left his wife and four children to fight in the war, his wife gave him a gold cross to wear around his neck for protection. After his family was murdered, Reuben set out on a path of revenge and for each person he killed—he would heat that cross up over a fire and then burn a scar into his flesh."

"Jesus, why?"

"It was his way of atonement I guess, Jessica." I stood and stretched.

"How many scars did Eli Cobb have, Tom?"

"The reporter told my family that with the exception of his face and the soles of his feet and hands… every inch of his flesh was covered in burnt crosses, even between his toes."

"My God," Jessica whispered and brought her hand to cover her mouth as if we both were now apart of some blasphemous act. "Did the reporter ever write the book?"

"Actually, he was at my family's home to buy permission to print the book Reuben Judah had written about his life."

"Did your family give him the go ahead for publication?"

"They signed a release only after the reporter had made a hundred dollar donation to the church Reuben Judah started before the war."

"The same church your uncle Frank presides over I presume?" I nodded yes without speaking the word. "So did the reporter ever publish Reuben's book?"

"He never got the chance, Jessica."

"Why not?"

"He committed suicide two weeks after he returned to San Francisco."

"My God, what ever happened to the book?"

"No one knows for sure," I said, looking down to where Jessica sat cross legged and let that sentience wash over me, her face beautifully blurred and content.

"What's wrong, Tom?" she asked and I spoke before I could stop the words.

"Do you think I'm a good person?" Jessica laughed, then looked up to where I stood and shook her head. My eyes still upon her as if they were appealing for her to right the wrong of past haunts and unknown depravities.

"It's funny, but I wanted to ask you the same thing about myself... considering what you know about me."

"I don't know why I even said those words, Jessica."

"It's alright. I know you're a good person, Tom."

"How can you know when I don't know myself sometimes?"

"I know because around you, I feel—"

"Secure?" I asked, cutting her off. She smiled wider and nodded her head.

"Yeah, that's exactly what it is. How did you know?"

"I guess it's because I feel the same way when I'm around you."

Jessica lay back and propped herself up on her elbows. "I see in you what I see in a lot of the young boys in my class. Their fathers are alcoholics or addicted to meth and they have no home life. It's like they are small birds fallen from a nest and I feel like it's up to me to put them back, put them in a safe place so they'll grow up and maybe make a difference in their cat-crazed world because I took the time to care about them when it was needed most... Does that sound weird to you?"

"No... not at all, Jessica. If one of those kids grows up without having the scars of their childhood to guard, they will go a lot further in their adult lives because you took the time to make their bitter days a little better." I paused and pulled her head against my knee and stroked her cheek with my fingers. "You have that rare gift inside of you, just like what your father has been telling you all along... That's your greatness and you've touched it all along but you never understood what it was."

She pressed her lips against my hand and kissed my fingers. "What is my greatness?"

"You heal the scars of broken lives and you have the ability to make the pain go away, Jessica." I could feel wetness staining the back of my hand, the purity of her conscious contained in the salt of those tears.

"Thank you, Tom," she whispered and wiped her eyes then nudged me toward the darkness below the rock. "You better get started on that skillet because if it's not clean after I inspect it, you'll lose your privilege of being my teacher's pet tonight."

"So that's the way it is, you do the cooking and I'm stuck with the dirty dishes," I said and Jessica laughed.

"While you get the skillet cleaned in the creek, I'll open two more beers and I'll give you your desert."

"I can only imagine what my desert will be," I said and winked.

"It's nothing you haven't already had, but the setting and the mood will be much better this time," Jessica answered, handing me the grease stained skillet.

I broke a green chem-lite and worked my way back down the steep grade to the creek that wove a moonlit tapestry down the mountainside. I used wet sand and a handful of green leaves to scrub out the blackened cookware and started back up the slope when a scrabble of rocks sounded below my position. I stopped, senses tuning in and all other thoughts tuning out. Instantly alert as vigilant eyes and ears searched the nightscape for some breech within the security of my newfound world.

A gaggle of voices sounded from the darkness below me, I snuffed out the chem.-lite and shoved the cleaned skillet under a bank of leaves, then slid back into the undergrowth and listened.

"I can see a campfire or something up ahead by the Bee Rocks," a voice said.

"Quit talking so fucking loud, Bennie," a man replied harshly, lower but loud enough that I could hear what was said.

Three half-lit silhouettes stopped a few hundred yards from where I lay mummied up in the brush and then cambered around the bend in the stream like desert moths seeking some distant flame.

"Where do you think the fucker is?" a large man asked, then skipped his feet to some tune only he could hear.

"How in the fuck should I know, Bennie? I only know they weren't at the cabin, so they must be around this campsite."

"It might be someone else's camp, Jimmy."

"No, Cindy called me from the school and said she heard Jessica asking her dad over the phone if she could borrow his truck to take that bastard camping at the Bee Rocks." Jim Prichard looked at Eddie Marshall, his broken nose bandaged and eyes black as pirate souls. "Did you bring the fucking bat, Eddie?"

"Yeah, but what if they both jump in the truck and leave before we get there?"

"Bennie pushed a rock and some logs across the road, so they're trapped on the Bee Rocks for the night," Jim Prichard said, I could see his grin from the maddened glow of their flashlights. "And that means they're both fucked."

PART Fourteen: Way of the Goat

Finality

"Nothing will end war unless the people themselves refuse to go to war." Albert Einstein

I scrambled back up the slope and found Jessica stretched out in a lawn chair by the fire. She smiled when I came trotting across the flat rock. "Get ready to move," I told her.

"Not in the mood?" she quipped.

"Your ex-husband, his brother, and that other friend of theirs are hiding a couple hundred yards below these rocks." Jessica bolted to her feet and walked briskly to where I stood.

"They can't be... no one knew we were coming up here, Tom." Her earlier jape lost as reality now crept into focus.

"A woman named Cindy called from the school and told Jim Prichard you were bringing me up here." Jessica shook her head, tears welling up in her eyes.

"How did she," Jessica paused and then gritted her teeth. "Fucking Cindy was eavesdropping when I called my dad. It doesn't matter anyway, Jim's not supposed to harass me anymore. I have a restraining order against him and he knows that."

"Jim and his buddies aren't here for you, Jessica… They're here for me."

Jessica started moving towards the tent. "I can grab a few things and we'll load up in the truck and leave."

I looked at her and shook my head. "It's too late, they've already blocked the road with trees and rocks, Jess… I'd also say they have their vehicle parked in the road to block anyone from getting to us and to keep us from getting out of here. We're trapped." I looked to where Jessica's cell phone sat beside her chair, she seemed to read my thoughts and spoke before I could ask.

"There's no cell phone reception this far back in the mountains, Tom."

"Shit," I muttered, looking around and then back to where Jessica stood watching me, her eyes showing the fear that had now lined her face. "Do you know of somewhere you can hide, someplace that can't be seen or found, Jess?"

"There's a small cave just down from where I parked the truck. Why?"

I pulled the last three chem-lites from my rucksack and handed Jessica two and then stuck the remaining lite and my K-bar into the cargo pocket of my pants. "I want you to take these and go stay in that cave." Jessica shook her head no.

"Tom… please." I cut off her protest.

"Listen to me, Jessica. Those men are here for me and if I have to face them with you around, it will put me at a disadvantage."

"I won't be a disadvantage, I can talk to them. Jim won't listen but Eddie Marshall will, he only hangs around Jim and his brother because they have money."

"It won't matter, Jessica. They didn't come all this way to be talked out of anything, and if something happens, I will be forced to protect you while fighting to protect myself at the same time." Jessica was still shaking her head. "Listen to me, Jessica. Jim Prichard brought a baseball bat. And I don't think he brought it to whack balls off the Bee Rocks for amusement."

"Tom... please."

"Jessica," I snapped cutting her off. "I need to know you're safe, so go stay in that cave."

Jessica dropped her head and started shaking, tears pattering the rocks at her feet. I pulled her close and kissed the top of her head. "I'm sorry... so sorry, Tom. This is all my fault."

"It's not your fault, Jessica. Now make sure you toss a few pebbles into that cave before you crawl inside." Jessica looked up at me confused, tears staining her cheeks. I wiped the salty drops free with my thumb. "The stones will spook anything hiding inside the cave and force whatever it may be outside. Keep your head down so your eyes won't reflect light and pull some laurel over the opening for camouflage. Do you understand?" She nodded and started to leave when my voice stopped her. "I want you to whistle when you're safely inside so I can douse the fire and then you stay put. No matter what happens on these rocks, you stay where it's safe until you hear me call for you."

"And if you don't come for me?"

"Then it will mean that things didn't work out the way I'd hoped, so you'll need to stay there until daylight. After that, listen and make sure you don't hear voices or footsteps and then walk back to your dad's cabin and call the police."

I stood by the fire and opened a can of beer, then waited for Jessica's whistle that came from the darkness beyond like a haunted whippoorwill calling to some lost and defeated mate. I poured the beer over the fire and waited until the ashes settled down before crawling to the ledge that overlooked the spot where Jim Prichard and his band of revenge seekers waited.

"I say we forget this shit and head back into town," a voice whispered loud enough for me to hear, the deep valley funneling the conversation to where I sat perched and flattened like a rock lizard. "You know Jessica has a restraining order against you, Jim."

"Quit being so chickenshit, Eddie. Besides, if that bitch goes to Ben Cole, I already have an airtight alibi."

"You do?"

"I'll tell Ben Cole I was in Stuarts Draft drinking beer with my brother and our friend Eddie Marshall," Jim Prichard said and laughed.

"Maybe so, Jim… but that fucker she's with is crazy. You didn't see his eyes back at the Meadow Muffin when we got in that fight. There wasn't anything behind them, it was like he wasn't there and nothing else mattered to him except some weird need to kill one of us."

"Jimmy said his nose got broke because that Judah guy caught him off guard," Bennie Prichard said in his brother's defense.

"How the fuck would you know, Bennie? You weren't there so stay out of this. What I'm talking about is between me and Jim."

"If you want to leave so bad, start walking," Jim Prichard hissed at his friend and then all three men snuffed out their flashlights as if some preordained prophecy was about to commence. "Let's move slow and easy so we don't knock any rocks free or we'll start a fucking avalanche."

They walked out onto the rock plateau like wraiths born from some hellish nightmare, dark shadows that moved about our camp with some misconceived fluidity. "Little pig, little pig, let me in," Bennie Prichard whispered towards the tent, they laughed and flicked on their flashlights.

Eddie Marshall pulled back the flap and looked inside. "They're not here, Jim."

"No shit, Sherlock." Jim Prichard was pissed and waved the beam of his light in a wide sweeping arc. "They can't be far away."

"Fuck this shit, Jim. I don't like this at all, it gives me the creeps."

Jim Prichard started to reply when I stood up from the rockface.

"I think I would listen to him, Jim." They spun and all three beams of light hit me full on like I was center stage giving a recital. "I'm up here minding my own business and doing a little fishing. I don't want any trouble."

"Where's Jessica?" asked Jim.

"She went to Baltimore with a bunch of teachers."

"Bullfuckingshit," Jim Prichard said loudly. "I know for a fact she came up here with you."

"I don't know what else to tell you... she's not here."

"Give me the bat." Eddie Marshall looked at his friend and started to protest, but was cut off. "You either give me that fucking bat or I'll have Bennie throw your sorry ass off this Goddamn cliff."

I kept the K-bar knife cupped in one hand and the fishing spear in the other. "Let's talk about this, Jim. What happened at the restaurant was my fault and I was charged for what I did and paid my fine. Now let's just drop this nonsense before someone gets hurt," I offered. The youngest Prichard laughed.

"He's a fraidy cat, Jimmy, just like you said," Bennie sang the words and tapped his toes like an excited kid.

"You and Eddie look around for Jessica," Jim spoke to his brother and began advancing towards me with the bat cradled on his shoulder.

Bennie Prichard looked at his brother and grinned like a fiend. "What are you gonna do to him, Jimmy?"

"I'm going to break this motherfucker's legs," he answered as I brought the tip of my spear up. "What the fuck do you think you're gonna do with that stick?"

Instead of answering, I waited for Jim Prichard to hesitate and then I snagged his shirt with the spear tip, then used both hands to twist the stave like I was wringing out a rag. The prongs of the spear wound tight around his shirt, causing him to drop the bat and grab the shank with both hands. I pulled forward until he was off balance and then spun the man in a half-circle like a pendulum. Jim Prichard lost his balance and fell, then began a slow arcing slide towards the never ending darkness of the ledge, his hands clawing at the smooth rockface like he were warding off some spell of doom cast upon him. And then Jim Prichard's face winked oddly out of the light as he disappeared from sight with a scream trapped in his throat. The sound of his body breaking upon the rocks below like that of a diseased and beach-ripened crab being crushed free of its sundried hull.

Bennie Prichard began dancing up and down, his mongoloid head bobbing while his cartoonish arms wove the air in a grotesque soliloquy, his antics both morbid and out of place for the tragic deed at hand, as if he were some macabre jester brought forth to survey the wretched scene.

Eddie Marshall pulled the younger Prichard away from the cliff's edge, both men crying and stumbling away from the campsite on wobbly legs. Jessica emerged from the darkness with both hands to her face, covering her eyes and shaking her head as if the gesture itself would fleece away the horrible event that had unfolded before her. I broke open the chem-lite and dropped it to the rocks below, then looked over the edge to where Jim Prichard had fallen.

Jessica's ex-husband lay as he had landed, crushed and broken on the rocks with his misshapen arms and legs twisted in wreckage like the boneless manacles of some obscene beast. Jim Prichard's blood began to stain the stones in crimson and purplish shadows that etched the greenish and ghastly scene of sorrows. Blood and stone, the mortar of life itself, all of mankind's past miseries and tragedies were written in blood and immortalized with stone effigies.

I stood looking down at the broken man and realized that, like a final leaf clinging to barren and wintered limbs, I was solitary to the exposure of Jim Prichard's death. I just wanted out of myself at that point, to stop my brain's overdrive—jump from this train of doom and destiny to float somewhere beyond my eternity of self loathing fate.

"Is he?' Jessica started to ask, walking forward. She was shaking and crying. I held up my hand and stopped her.

"Don't come over here, Jessica. He's gone... and it's my fault."

"It's not your fault, Tom. You tried to talk him out of this."

"And who will believe that, Jessica? His brother and Eddie Marshall are headed straight for the sheriff and I'll be charged with murder."

"It was an accident, I was a witness and I'll testify that you—" I cut Jessica off before she could finish.

"No one saw you, Jessica." She looked at me, confused, shaking as tears slid down her face. "You were hiding and no one knew you were here except me... and Ben Cole has already let it be known where he stands, so it's a case of my word against theirs and who do you think they're going to believe—the local boys or the unemployed stranger?"

"What do we do, Tom?

"Take your cell phone and get in the truck and leave, Jessica."

"What about you?"

"I'll work my way down to his body and see if there's anything I can do, then I'll backtrack out to the road and meet you at the spot where they piled up the rock and trees. After I clear the roadblock, you call your dad once you get in an area that gives you cell phone reception and let him know what happened."

Jessica came over and buried her head in my chest and started crying harder, deep racking sobs that seemed to free something inside of me. "What are you going to do, Tom?"

I stroked the top of her head, her hair had the smell of laurel blooms and wood smoke. "I'll walk the rest of the way to your father's cabin and wait there for the police. I need time to think this thing out." I pushed Jessica back and looked at her face, for one door that closes another one will open. I kissed her forehead and forced a smile. "Everything's going to be alright, Jessica."

"Promise?" she asked, wiping her eyes.

"I give you my wink of love on it," I said and winked.

I dropped off the slope to where the greenish hue lit Jim Prichard's body like a flare, and the sight of that ghastly illumination led me backwards to a time and place I could not escape. I wondered at that point if a man could not write his own demise from such a jilted and forlorn memory.

Johnson was waiting in our billets when my platoon returned from the mess hall. "We'll be having an observer with us on our patrol tonight," he explained as we filed inside. The men groaned.

"Who?" I asked.

"Captain Benson."

"Why in the fuck is that ass clown tagging along?" someone asked.

"At ease with that shit. Dr. Feelgood will be accompanying our patrol as a non-combatant, as an unarmed observer only. But he is still an officer in the United States Marine Corps and every swinging dick here will show him the proper respect," Johnson answered and nodded in my direction. "Corporal Judah will be my second in command and act as our point man when we move out. Are there any questions?"

"No, sir," we sounded off as one.

"Good. Squad leaders start getting your men squared away and prepare to move out a half hour before dark. This is going to be a night patrol to a pre-selected ambush position, so make sure all your night vision devices have fresh batteries." I started to walk away when Johnson stopped me. "I need a word with you, Lazarus."

"Yes, Sergeant." Johnson put his arm around my shoulder and steered me clear of the other men.

"You know Dr. Feelgood is only coming along because of you?"

"Why me, Sergeant?"

"Because he wants you out of my platoon and shipped back to the states," Johnson grinned, then leaned close and whispered in my ear. "It would be tough shit if one of those sand fuckers got a lucky shot it in and tagged Dr. Feelgood."

"Benson has a hard on for me," I said.

"Dr. Feelgood has a hard on for both of us."

"Why?"

"Because you and I are the perfect killers," he said and winked. "Go ahead and grab your gear, then meet me out front with the rest of the platoon."

We moved through the ruins of the inner city red zones where vacant buildings sat littered with pock-marked holes from small arms fire. Lights blinked out as we advanced on cautious feet while vigilant eyes searched the shadows, muffled sounds coming from the darkened ruins like ghosts summoning the living to join the dead in their unknown games.

"There's been a lot of contact with the Hajis in this area, so we're going to pull into a secure ambush position and watch for any activity. Squad leaders, pair your men up in groups of two and no fucking sleeping, if you get drowsy, yoke an arm behind your back," Johnson ordered and then looked at me. "You and I will share a position, Lazarus."

"What about me?" asked Benson.

"You wanted to see what the real shit was like so find a secure location down front along on the ambush line." Dr. Feelgood hesitated, then shuffled off into the gloom like a lost soul in search of a host.

"What a dumbfuck," Johnson laughed as we dropped to the ground behind a slab of ruptured concrete, burnt cars like robotic skeletons in the moonlight as the men to our front dropped into positions as if the ground itself had swallowed them whole.

"It's down to me and you, Lazarus," Johnson said with a yawn. I looked at him and squinted. "We're all that's left of the original Prophets of Ruin," he explained.

"You ever wonder why?"

"Because we were bred for it; we're the supreme warriors and the ultimate survivors."

"Why do you like it so much, Sergeant?"

"Like what so much?" he asked and lit two cigarettes, handing me one.

"War," I replied, taking a drag.

"Don't give me that shit, Lazarus. You like it just as much as I do, I can see it in that fucked up eye of yours so don't try and hide behind God and all that other shit you're always preaching about. You and I are like a set of abnormal twins looking at our reflection," he said and exhaled twin jets of smoke from his nose like snake fangs. I shook my head and exhaled through my nose. He noticed the mirrored movement and laughed.

"You see," he said and grinned like a maddened reprobate. My multi-colored eye twitched but remained open in odd defiance.

"That's not exactly true, Sergeant Johnson."

"Bullshit," he laughed. "Men like us love war and we love it for the same reason."

"What reason is that?"

"You already know the answer to that question." He looked at me and smiled. "What was the name of that fucking hick town you're from?"

"Waynesboro, Virginia."

"You take all the books out of every library, all the magazines and newspapers and everything else that was ever written and burn it. Let that redneck hellhole you're from sit abandoned for five hundred years and see what you have left," he said and snuffed the cigarette on his palm. "You come back after five hundred years and all the buildings and houses would be gone, but the statues and monuments will weather for all time, marble sculptures of great men forever young and etched in stone, warriors and empire builders who conquered nations with an undying lust for war. That's why we love it Lazarus. It comes down to immortality. Men like you and me want our names carved in stone... we want our names remembered for all eternity."

"There's got to be more to it than that, Sergeant... at least there is for me."

"You can't bullshit the bullshitter, Lazarus." I didn't want to believe what he was saying, but I could not offer a protest. "Aren't you a little curious as to how I knew you and I were alike?"

"How did you know?"

"You're always smiling when we're in a combat firefight. And you're smiling because you like the killing as much as I do."

"Thinking that you might be a murderer doesn't bother you?" I asked.

"I don't see it as murder, Lazarus."

"How can you see it any other way?"

"I see it as a chance to exterminate an odd and macabre race of pests and that's why I'm called the Goat... I am the alpha and the omega, the first and the last. I am the perfect killer for the job and so are you."

A round cracked to our front and the ambush line opened up, tracer rounds sped through the night like demon fireflies before winking out to some unknown oblivion beyond the realm of darkness. Squad leaders began directing fire down front as I picked up to move forward, sighting in with my weapon at the ready. Johnson put a hand on my shoulder and pulled me back to the ground. "Not yet," he whispered, flicking the safety off on his weapon.

A sudden whoosh sounded and the night erupted into daylight as a greenish flare exploded overhead, parachute dropping the burning orb to the ground like a falling angel. Captain Benson ran toward us, bent over as if the rounds would miss his hunkered down frame. Johnson never said a word and fired one round that blew out the left side of Benson's throat, sending the man face first into the ground. Men were yelling for the medic from other positions as Johnson pulled me to my feet and we both ran towards our right flank and away from the grisly scene. *"Dr. Feelgood just became Dr. Feelbad," Johnson chuckled as we ran.*

"Captain Benson is hit," a voice yelled.

Johnson and I came from the opposite direction to where Captain Benson lay in the gray stitches of death below the waning light of the flare. "Anyone see what happened?" Johnson asked. The men gathered around shook their heads.

"I saw him pick up to my right and start moving towards the rear when he went down. I didn't pay much attention because I thought he probably tripped and fell," I said.

Johnson sighed and nodded. "I tried to tell the stupid fucker that going on a night patrol without a weapon would get him killed."

"He should have fucking listened," someone said as the medic pulled the dog tags free of his fractured neck.

"Too late now," Johnson answered, then looked towards the other men. "Squad leaders, check your men and give me a head count. Once you get Dr. Feelgood tagged and bagged, go ahead and radio in that we have a KIA, Doc." The medic nodded and unzipped the black rubberized bag and slid it under Captain Benson's corpse. "Let headquarters know the KIA is Captain Michael C. Benson."

Captain Benson's hat lay on the ground at my feet. I snatched it up and shoved it into my cargo pocket as our platoon began moving out.

I made it to the front porch of Clinton Spire's cabin and found Jessica sitting with her head cradled in her hands. "Did you make the calls, Jessica?" She nodded without looking up.

"I got the number you dialed off my cell phone and called your dad, Tom. He said you've been considered missing without permission from a VA hospital for over two weeks and you're supposed to be taking prescribed medication every day."

"I'm not going back to that hospital, Jessica. Not ever."

"Tom, your dad said you needed to be in that hospital and right now he and your uncle Frank are on their way here to help us take care of things."

"I can't be in that hospital, everything's the same there. The same sad stories, the same whiny pill popping souls telling them and the same looks of false compassion from the counselors. When I was in that place, I was stagnate and dead to the world. The only time I have felt alive these past three years is when I'm with you, Jessica. You got to believe me," I said as her cell phone rang. She answered and mumbled something I could not hear and clicked the flap shut.

"That was dad. Sheriff Cole and two deputies are at the house. They want you and me there for questioning, Tom."

"You go on ahead, Jessica. I need to pack a few things and then I'll head up to your house in a bit."

"It would be better if we went together, Tom." I shook my head.

"I know, Jessica. Just give me a little time, I really need it right now." She stood and hugged me tighter than she ever had, as if she were trying to meld our bodies into one infinite being. We kissed lightly, a kiss in search of a kiss to find and rekindle some passion yet conceived.

"Are you alright, Tom?" I forced a smile and she seemed to be put at ease.

"Better than alright. I'm as close to perfect as I'll ever be."

"Okay, I'll tell the sheriff you haven't made it back yet," she said and then looked me in the eye with a strange fierceness. "I love you, Tom Judah."

With those words, something opened up inside me. I wanted to know Jessica Spire, wanted to know what lay behind the blue eyes with those small gold flecks. I wanted to be there and to help her heal those stress fractures in her life, to be the protector and savior when she needed it most.

I kissed her and stroked her cheek with my hand. "I love you too, Jessica Spire. Now get going before they come looking for you."

She nodded and held my hand until she dropped off the last step of the porch and let her palm slowly slide free as if our fingers willed no escape. I realized as she walked away that I had spoken the words of love before my brain had allowed them to form. It was the first and last honest emotion I would ever feel. And to feel the touch of that perfection once, to hold love and what it represents inside living and breathing flesh made everything right with the world.

Jessica had long gone and I let the vacant span of time wander with raping servitude as my bitter and desperate world crumbled. Nothing sounded or moved while the deep shadows of the tree line crept in their slinking way towards the driveway. I sat by the open door of the cabin and sharpened two staves into crude spears, then looked out the window; the far limestone ridges of the Bee Rocks seemed to jut from the mountains like grey scars or perhaps the backs of giant beasts rising from some alien and underground place. I opened my laptop and began writing what was needed and left the unanswered questions to those who would have the courage to seek them out.

Sergeant Johnson's voice yelled from his office, "Lazarus, get your grubby ass in here."

"Yes, Sergeant."

I stepped to his desk and snapped to parade rest, arms yoked tight behind my back. "At ease, Lazarus." I relaxed my arms to Johnson's grin. "I've looked over a report that Dr. Benson wrote on you before he got wacked. Do you know what it said?"

"No, Sergeant."

"It said you're suffering from shell shock. Post Traumatic Stress Disorder brought on by a fractured identity." He sighed and rubbed his eyes. "I don't like this kinda bullshit. They send men over here and expect them to become the perfect killers fighting the good fight, Prophets of Ruin doing their job of killing bad guys for pay and chow.

But the first time they show signs of liking it, liking what they were trained to do, they want us to turn that switch off and make things right."

"I understand, Sergeant."

"I don't think you do, Tom." He used my given name. I'd almost forgotten that part of me. I was 'Lazarus' to the original Prophets of Ruin. I was the one who had risen from the smoke and ashes, the odd-eyed messiah called forth from death's crusty grip as a combat Phoenix reborn into the perfect killer. "They're giving you a discharge, son."

"I don't understand, Sergeant. What'd I do wrong? I followed your rules."

"You didn't do a fucking thing wrong in my eyes, but they're giving you a one way ticket home with medals on your chest and blood on your hands," Johnson said.

"When?"

"End of the week, son. I'm sorry as hell about this because you're the perfect Marine and I was proud to serve with you." Johnson pinched the bridge of his nose. He was missing the tip of his index finger on his right hand. I hadn't noticed that before, odd. "Once you get stateside, they want you to check into a VA hospital for further evaluation. All the instructions will be in your discharge orders."

"That's it... just like that?"

"Yup, you're going home and for the rest of us, it's just another day in paradise."

"Has all the blood and killing ever once made you feel guilty, Sergeant?"

He shook his head and said, "I want you to remember this because guilt ain't anything but the truth in disguise, and every time I send another one of these sand niggers to hell, I could shit sunshine and tap dance on rainbows. Son, when you saw your first fire fight, that first kill was a fear kill—you were in a world of shit, wondering if you were gonna lose life or limb and you reacted the way you were trained through the fog and noise. You smoked some worthless sand nigger and you were right to do so in my eyes, but you will always remember your first kill and it will color how you act in the future. Some men enjoy the rush of killing and it will become a drug to them—they're the cowboys. Cowboys are alright in my unit, but I would rather they become what I call the professionals. Professionals acquire neither satisfaction nor regret from killing—for them, it is a mission that needs to be completed, nothing more and nothing less. The professionals will return home and sleep like babies and live out their lives successfully and satisfied in the knowledge that they performed admirably in very difficult times. It's just another day in paradise to the professionals. Finally, some men become the guilters. They will carry the weight of killing with them and it will increase exponentially with every mission. I have no room for guilters in my unit. The rest of their lives will be lived a world of shit and they will never recover from the necessities of their actions. The guilt will eat them from the inside until only a scar of their life remains. To avoid becoming a guilter, we harden ourselves through training and discipline. This is a beautiful fucking world—we are Marines, and we make our own rules in combat like we always have."

"Which one am I, Sergeant, a cowboy, professional, or a guilter?"

"You're the most dangerous one of all, Lazarus—you're all three."

It took that final memory of Sergeant Johnson to awaken my beliefs about war and its aftermath. I have lived through both and damned each of them equally. There are places in our world where the questions of our existence are lived without answers, where peace is not an absolute but a rare gift from a frozen and unvoiced God. It was man who drew the first breath and within that exchange of air, he created a tabernacle of depravity between all men. The first rock thrown in anger gave birth to a new dominion over the world and those men who understood the power of that conflict were insane and without amnesty. The tossing of that single stone gave rise to war and all soldiers of this world both then and now shall one day stand in judgment before the meek. But warfare itself will endure without surrendering to such a verdict and no decree will ever right the wrong of it.

Once you have faced the hostilities of combat you come to understand that no one dies in a conflict for their country; men are killed because of the wanton acts of revenge or power and parallel lives are devastated by those immoral actions. Old men covet warfare and they crave the bitter tang of battle while standing guard over the dead as vendors without prayer or salvation. The men who fight and die in wars are made promises behind words like honor, duty, and perseverance, but a solider ultimately understands that the secret validity of those pledges are nothing more than lies in disguise.

I knew this to be true and was looking at my screensaver when the sheriff's voice boomed through a megaphone, asking for me to come out unarmed with my hands empty. I kept looking at the laptop's picture of those young Marines who were nothing more than ghostly faces staring back with their wind-burned lips and raptor smiles, prophets of ruin forever young and captured in a time and place when violent young men ruled their hard and callow world. A breeze blew a faint scent through the open window, so subtle, some reeking odor of my past that I could not place.

The sheriff called out again with his ultimatum of a peaceable surrender or the option of being taken into custody by force. I left the laptop open to the captured picture and walked out into the cool shade of the yard with my spears and knife held ready for their action. The three officers were talking to me, but their words were lost. My blue-brown eye was twitching as I stood rooted to my controlled and delivered destiny, watching the men and waiting for their action of fate, waiting for their shift of attention, that slight relaxation, the hesitation that would flick the final switch...

EPILOGUE

The Final Word

"If you want a happy ending it depends on where you stop your story." Orson Welles

Tri-City Gazette

Stuarts Draft, Virginia

Staff Writer

The six day investigation into the accidental homicide of a local man has found that ex-Marine, Thomas Kendall Judah acted alone in the events surrounding the deadly dispute. James Edward Prichard's body was found below a rock ledge in the George Washington National Forrest where he had fallen after an altercation with the suspect. An earlier argument between Mr. Judah and James Prichard led the authorities to a small cabin where the suspect was staying, a disagreement between law enforcement officers and Mr. Judah ensued and the ex-Marine was fatally shot.

The Commonwealth's attorney office declined to press charges against neither Sheriff Ben Cole nor his two deputies into the shooting death of Mr. Judah, saying: "He was told to drop his weapons several times and when Deputy Alvin Spitler holstered his side arm to place the

suspect in custody, Mr. Judah charged the officer with his weapons brandished."

The fatal shooting took place near the wilderness area of Back Creek where Mr. Judah died on the scene in what the Commonwealth Attorney has ruled suicide by cop.

Henna Van Buren, a personal assistant to the Prichard family, issued this brief statement to reporters: "Everyone is in shock and the family asks that they be allowed to mourn while officials continue their investigation into this tragedy."

Mike Judah, father of the suspect (Tom Judah), and another family member arrived in Stuarts Draft yesterday from their homes in Waynesboro to assist authorities in their investigation. At a scheduled press conference, Mr. Judah told reporters about his son's struggles since returning from the war in Iraq. "Tom was discharged from the Marines after serving thirty-two months over there and what came home wasn't the son that left." Mr. Judah became visibly shaken when he answered questions about the war and his son, "Tom saw a lot of his friends die in Iraq and he carried that pain with him on the inside. He refused to talk about it and would generally clam up or become verbally combative when someone would bring up the issue."

According to state forensic investigators working with the local police, Mr. Judah has confirmed that a laptop computer recovered from the rustic shack belonged to his son. Early reports from the discovery have revealed that the computer contained an explanation into these events in the form of a chaptered and book-length manifesto. The computer, as well as a single military dog tag belonging to one Clifford R. Danko, an MP3 player with the name "Frag" engraved across the back, sunglasses, a single piece of hard candy sold commercially as "Fireballs," and a military cap bearing the rank of captain was sent to Richmond for further forensic analysis. "Test results of those articles and any additional evidence recovered on the computer won't be known for several weeks," investigators said.

A statement issued by the U.S. State Department confirmed that Thomas K. Judah was discharged from the Marine Corps near the end of his third tour of duty in Iraq for medical reasons. A department spokesman verified that Thomas Kendall Judah, a decorated Marine, suffered from severe Post Traumatic Stress Disorder and was being treated as an inpatient at a regional Veteran's Hospital. According to military records provided by the U.S. Government, Thomas K. Judah rose to the rank of Lance Corporal and was awarded the Bronze Star with a V device for valor, two citations for wounds received in combat (Purple Heart), and several other medals for accomplishment and distinction.

"All in all, he was the perfect Marine," a spokesman for the department said by phone.

American news agency MSNBC reported earlier this year: "Nearly one in 10 American combat personnel who served in Iraq were diagnosed with Post Traumatic Stress Disorder, most after witnessing death or participating in combat," according to a Pentagon study that could add fodder to a budget battle in Congress over veterans' health care. *Overall, the study found more than a third of U.S. servicemen required psychological counseling after returning from Iraq.*

"Nineteen percent met the military's risk criteria for a mental health concern such as post traumatic stress or depression. That's compared to 11.3 percent among veterans who served in Afghanistan and 8.5 percent from deployments elsewhere," according to a report published in the Journal of the American Medical Association.

Studies conducted by the National Institute of Mental Health have concluded:

"People with PTSD may startle easily, become emotionally detached (especially in relation to people with whom they used to be close), lose interest in things they used to enjoy, have trouble feeling affectionate, be irritable, and become more aggressive or even physically violent. They avoid situations that remind them of the original incident and anniversaries of the incident are often very difficult. PTSD symptoms seem to be worse if the event that triggered them was deliberately initiated by another person, as in combat where the individual witnessed or participated in killing and must use physical violence to protect themselves. Most people with PTSD repeatedly relive the trauma in their thoughts during the day and experience nightmares when they sleep. These are referred to as flashbacks. Flashbacks may consist of images, sounds, smells, or feelings and are often triggered by ordinary occurrences such as the pop of a balloon or a car backfiring on the street. A person having a flashback may lose touch with reality, even

with their eyes open, and believe that the traumatic incident is happening all over again."

Mike Judah, also a veteran of war (Vietnam), confirmed those reports, adding, "Tom waited six months after returning home after his first tour before he could get an appointment with VA counselors. I saw the same kind of red tape and I exhibited similar aggressive behavior when I came home after serving in Vietnam."

In an exclusive interview with the Tri-City Gazette, Mr. Judah said that his son's decline began thirteen days after being admitted into the VA hospital, when he received news that his Platoon Sergeant (Anthony Earl Johnson) was killed in a roadside bomb attack. "My son thought the world of Sergeant Johnson. He had said on numerous occasions that as a Marine, Johnson was the greatest of all time. After Tom learned of Sergeant Johnson's death, he convinced the VA therapist to allow him a leave of absence to attend Johnson's funeral in Los Angeles."

Mr. Judah cried softly, saying his son had become manic-compulsive about healing his combat experiences and inner scars by himself. "I was hoping Tom would attend the funeral to clear his head and come home better than what he was when he left."

Investigators confirmed through Veterans Administration doctors and Mr. Judah that his son had stopped taking his prescribed depression medicine last month because he (Tom) said it made him feel "nothing." After interviewing several local doctors on the side effects of depression medicine, each physician confirmed that prescribed *medication such as Prozac, Paxil, and Lexapro used to treat depression come with side effects, some of which may be adverse.*

"Many patients who stop taking their anti-depressant medication without a doctor's guidance will experience suicidal thoughts, nightmares, semi-psychotic episodes, and violent paroxysms," said one area physician.

Sheriff Cole seemed distraught, but summed up his thoughts on the investigation with this statement: "It doesn't matter what was written on the computer. Whatever prompted Tom Judah to act out in such a violent manner went with him to his grave. That's the part of this that will remain unsolved and unanswered. We may never know."

Simon Archer closed the lid on my laptop and looked across the table at me. "Are you sure this manuscript is it…the whole thing?"

"It's as pure and authentic as the day he typed it, Simon. I copied the entire manuscript file right off Tom Judah's actual computer. Tom actually named the document, 'Scars of the Prophet' after his great grandfather."

"Reuben Judah?" he asked.

"The very same."

Simon stood up and placed the palms of his hands on the table then leaned forward, as if he were about to chastise me. But this was an opportunity to earn out and Simon Archer could smell anything that would benefit him and make his investors money. "How in the Hell did you manage to copy Tom Judah's manuscript right off his personal computer."

"The news media had total television coverage but I was the first investigative journalist from a major magazine to start asking questions. The sheriff told me I couldn't see the laptop at first, but once I started quoting the Freedom of Information Act and what our lawyers would do to him and his reelection campaign. He finally caved in and let me look over the open document in an office without a phone or an internet connection." I grinned and pulled out the flash drive I wore like a necklace. "I got the deputy watching me to grab us some coffee and then it was just a matter of right clicking and copying the document from Tom Judah's laptop before the officer got back."

"Nice…and a nice touch ending the piece with the local newspaper article." Simon smiled then clasped his hands behind his head and stretched. "But I don't know how we'll be able to run the story until the evidence is released by the police." I nodded and pulled an envelope from the breast pocket of my coat.

"The Commonwealth has officially closed the case so I arranged for Mike Judah to sign over all North American rights to his son's story… Everything you've read belongs to the magazine, Simon."

"What did that cost us?"

"You're not going to believe me," I said with a smile.

"Ten thousand?" he asked.

"I got everything for a hundred dollar donation to his brother's Pentecostal church."

"Nothing else…That's it?" Simon laughed.

"That's it," I said offering the document across the table. Simon went to take the contract but I pulled the envelope back out of his reach. "There's more…I also have the rights to the manuscript supposedly written by Reuben Judah."

"How much extra did that cost the magazine?"

"It was included in the original donation of a hundred dollars," I said finally handing him the contract.

Simon looked at me and clasped his hands as if in prayer. "Wilbur Grisham is retiring next year and if these articles of yours boost our circulation it'll look good when we promote someone to our next managing editor. Where is the Reuben Judah manuscript?"

"I used some of my old college contacts and tracked the manuscript down…and you're not going to believe this." Simon looked at me, greedy eyes and anticipation etched across his face. "It's in San Francisco in the care of a male nurse that cared for Reuben Judah until the day he died."

"No shit."

"No shit, Simon."

"I want you to make all the necessary travel arrangements and be on the first plane from New York to San Francisco…I want that manuscript."

I pulled out a single airline ticket from my breast pocket. "I already have, I leave tomorrow morning and I've already made a pre-arranged appointment with the nurse."

"You pull this off and the managing editor job is yours," Simon replied and gave me a thumbs up.

It was what I wanted most in life, advancement, position and authority. Simon knew this...and he had me hooked with that baited desire. "I'll do my best, Simon."

Sometimes what you crave most unravels the very fabric of your life, what I wanted out of life was placed before me on a journalistic platter like some reeking and undeserved reward. But nothing is ever as it seems, every reward has a price. I plucked the strings of time and found out through Reuben Judah that certain lives echo beyond eternity...

FORTHCOMING

The Prophet of Cobb Hollow

Mingo Kane

July 2011

San Francisco

Paul Tandy opened his sallow and deadpan eyes. The frailness of his thin and wasted body outlined beneath the sterile hospital sheets, tubes ran like disturbing tentacles from his emasculated arms to a host of beeping monitors. He punched the button on his morphine drip, a trained and starving parasite clinging to its dying host as the fragile life force slipped by.

"Please forgive me should I begin to wander, opiates do have such lucid effects," he apologized with a tight smile, already riding the narcotic buzz ever closer to that absolute infinity he fought against.

"I understand," I answered.

A nurse in white scrubs came in and checked the monitors and IV drip. Death's white clad helpers, debt collectors until all accounts are paid in full. He watched the woman go about her clipboard duties and waited until she left the room before he continued.

"Mr. Reuben said someone would come, wanting to know about him and his life," he paused and shifted in his bed. "I think that is partly why Reuben asked to be cremated when he passed."

"So they…or rather a nosy writer like me wouldn't seek out his grave?" The dying man gave a soft laugh and shook his head no.

"Actually, it was only after he gave me the manuscript and I read his final will is when I found out about the request for cremation. Mr. Reuben wrote that he might as well fan the fires now rather than face the Hell of his eternity later."

"Mr. Reuben sounds like he was a hard man," I said and smiled down at him. He looked towards the window and nodded slightly.

"In some ways he was and yet Mr. Reuben had an odd compassion about him that drew you in."

"Such as?"

"Even way back then, everyone suspected what I was."

"That you are a homosexual?" I cut in. A sheepish smile slipped across his face.

"How did you know?"

"I have connections and did some research before I contacted you. I knew that while Mr. Judah was at the hospital, he would only allow you to care for him towards the end of his life, and only you knew his real name was not Luther Eli Cobb."

"Considering what I am...I suppose that delicious sliver of information strikes you as odd?"

"I'll admit knowing what little I know about Reuben Judah, it does pose some unanswered questions...Is this the hospital where Mr. Judah stayed?" I asked changing the subject.

"Oh my, no. This is a private hospice that caters to the wealthy upper crust of our shrinking society. Mr. Reuben was confined to a state facility where I was employed, a truly dreadful place. But, since Mr. Reuben had no known living relatives and lived under the assumed name of Luther Eli Cobb, he was placed there as an inmate of the state until his death."

I looked around the room where framed art work adorned the papered walls, lacquered floors were spotless and the staff was neatly dressed and courteous—a final passing of the empty offering plate where the patients have nothing to ante up, fares and tares when facing the sterility of death's cold grip. The karma cup is empty. No gold coin this time around, my friend...a final roll of the dice for old times.

"How can you afford?"

"To be here instead of a community hospital?" He cut in letting a thin slice of his tongue slide across those pale and waxen lips, almost as if he were tasting, or perhaps testing the answer he was about to give. "Shall we say that here in San Francisco I made certain lifelong friends with connections both political and otherwise. In my younger days I catered to powerful men who had secret desires in their guarded lives, so therefore I was taken care of for my innate ability to keep quiet their petty indiscretions."

"I see," I replied and smiled in spite of myself. I liked this frail man, his demeanor was petite and it had me thinking maybe that was why Reuben Judah trusted this delicate fellow. He had come from a time when you had to keep secrets if you were to survive in a masculine world that frowned upon the dissimilar.

"You know we haven't been properly introduced," he said holding out his feminine hand. I took the offered hand and shook, the bones beneath the porcelain skin like that of a fragile child.

"I'm Martin Carlson…the journalist from New York," I replied.

"Martin is a name Mr. Reuben admired greatly. Of course you already know I am Paul Tandy."

"I'm curious, why did Mr. Judah like that particular name?"

"The name Martin is derived from Mars." I looked down at him lost in the translation. "Mars was the Roman God of War," he explained.

"Paul, weren't you ever the least bit frightened of Reuben Judah?"

"Why Heavens, no. Mr. Judah treated me kindly when the rest of the world sought to do otherwise. As I said earlier, he had an odd compassion about him…In some ways I loved him like a father, queer as that may sound," he said.

"So tell me, Paul. What did you find so compassionate about Mr. Reuben?"

"Compassion it was, but before I regale you with my explanation would you be so kind as to provide me with a sip of water? Morphine is such a wonderful drug but it leaves me terribly parched." I took the container and held it to his pallid lips and watched as Paul Tandy took a shallow sip through the straw.

"Do you want another drink, Mr. Tandy?"

"No, and please call me Paul, I feel we're almost friends now that we have made the proper introductions."

"Okay, you were telling me about Reuben's generous side."

He smiled at my choice of words. "I am not sure generous is the word I would use, but perhaps it does apply in a strange way. It was 1946 when I was first employed at the state mental asylum and found myself in the care of Mr. Reuben and other veterans suffering from post war shell shock. I was warned about him of course, he had already served a number of years by that time. He was a condemned prisoner to that institution, you see, an inmate for life… incarcerated for strangling a man to death with his bare hands."

"You mean outright murder?"

"Not exactly, apparently some poor soul tried to rob Reuben and our dear Mr. Judah took exception to that indecent foray. During his court proceeding the appointed district attorney made the argument that Reuben had acted with excessive and with undue force and therefore he sought a 2nd degree murder conviction. This was before the court system had metal detectors and pat down searches of course. I believe it was the local papers that wrote—at that point, Mr. Luther Eli Cobb sprayed the court and district attorney with gasoline and then struck a match to both."

"Was the attorney killed?"

"No, but his legs were burned to a point that he was confined to a wheelchair. It took six months to repair the court room and by that time Mr. Reuben was declared legally insane and therefore committed."

"And that's your idea of compassion, Paul?"

"No, that is how Reuben came to be at the asylum, his compassion is what he did for me...a deed begat of trust, and in return...he earned my confidence. Quid pro quo, Martin." He closed his eyes briefly and then reopened them and asked for another sip of water.

"If you don't feel up to this I can return tomorrow when you have had more time to rest," I said as he drank. He shook his head and then swallowed before he spoke.

"Ask for me tomorrow and ye shall find me a grave man. Do you know where that particular quote originated?"

"Mercutio talking about his pending death from Shakespeare's, Romeo and Juliet," I replied.

"Bravo...I am impressed, well done indeed, Martin. Now, where was I? I am afraid the morphine has begun to sink the fangs of lethargy into my failing revival of thoughts."

"Reuben did something for you and in turn you did something for him."

"Oh yes, I was at that dreadful asylum less than a week when an inmate by the name of David Allen Macy attacked me. He was a convicted molester of children and a very nasty man, of course the brutish lout tried to rape me but several orderlies were able to pull him off before that unpleasant incident occurred. Mr. Reuben had a great distaste for this oafish beast and that night the gruesome pedophile apparently hung himself with a belt. The odd thing was, Mr. Macy did so from his door knob and he was found in the sitting position on the floor with no pressure on his crushed neck from the noose. No one neither cared nor investigated the matter, and the suicide was quickly put to rest and the body donated to a local college as medical fodder for dissection."

"I'm lost, Paul. How did this bond you and Reuben Judah?"

"It was Reuben's belt that Mr. Macy had supposedly used to hang himself. Of course I knew Mr. Judah had actually enacted the dastardly deed himself and only doctored the scene to make it appear as a suicide."

"You saw him kill Mr. Macy?" He shook his head.

"No...actually I did not witness the crime."

"Then how can you be sure, Paul?"

"I let Reuben use my Zippo lighter as he explained how he used his bare hands to crush the throat of Mr. Macy. I watched as he heated a gold cross and then used it to burn a scar across the back of his hand. I kept quiet about what Mr. Reuben had confessed to me and a friendship was born of that bloody trust." Paul Tandy looked up to where I stood over him, our eyes met and he held my curious gaze. "You do know about the cross and those ghastly scars I presume?"

"I heard the rumors from a very distant relative but I could not confirm that aspect of Reuben Judah's legend."

"The scars were no legend I can assure you, Martin. In accordance with his will only I was permitted to wash and prepare Mr. Reuben's body for cremation."

"Did you count the number of scars Reuben had burnt into his skin, Paul?"

"It never occurred for me to try, dear fellow."

"Why?"

"Those hideous burn marks covered every inch of his body with the exception of his palms, face and the soles of his feet. The scars were actually quite small, the crucifix had a smaller raised cross of thin wire in the middle and he only heated that section. The fresh scars looked like the feet of shore birds, and the older scars were burnt in so many overlapping layers they had outstretched spines like sea urchins. Those hideous burns gave his skin a scaly look that almost seemed to shimmer and reflect light when the sun caught Mr. Reuben at the right angle."

"Jesus, he even had scars down there?" I said looking below my belt.

"Oh Lord no," Paul giggled, "Mr. Reuben was a prideful man and I can assure you there were no marks in that region. Even though he was thought to be 118 years old at the time, Mr. Reuben didn't look a day over fifty. Always exercising and even the crazies in that place knew when they first saw him, you left Mr. Reuben alone."

"They were scared of him?" He shook his head yes.

"Everyone was scared of Reuben Judah, even the staff."

"Everyone except you?" Paul smiled and nodded.

"Yes, everyone except me...If you messed with Mr. Reuben, bad things happened."

"What kind of bad things, Paul?"

"Mr. Reuben never raised his hand publicly to incarcerated inmates or the staff, but if one of those horrid convicts were to push Mr. Reuben or try to harm one of the weaker patients...that person would end up in a cast. Quite simple really. A slip in the shower, tripped over a shoe with a broken arm or leg as the result of their clumsiness. If one of the staff members got out of line with Mr. Reuben, they might find themselves audited by the IRS, or have their bank accounts frozen for some unknown reason. We all knew it was Mr. Reuben's doing but whenever I would ask him about it, he would only respond to my accusations by telling me the sheepdog protects his flock. Mr. Reuben was a very powerful man." Paul Tandy had now pulled me into a story I was eager to know and he could sense that excitement in me. "Be careful what you seek, Martin. Greed is such a hard emotion to wield, and it will ultimately possess what you are if you cannot control its pull," he cautioned. I placed my hand on his shoulder and gave it a squeeze.

"I'll be careful, Paul."

"Yes, we all start out as cautious creatures by nature...I was careful too, dear fellow. I told Mr. Reuben the same thing when he warned me about allowing greed to guide my heart. In the end Mr. Reuben knew what I wanted most of all and he dangled that prize before me like bait...of course I took everything Mr. Reuben had to offer and because of that, I was trapped by the secret jewels of my own desires. Mr. Reuben captured me like he captured everyone…he offered us the opportunity to taste our greed…he forced us to choose." Paul Tandy closed and eyes and exhaled his next statement like a whisper no one should hear…"In the end…I did him."

"Did what to him?"

"I killed Reuben Shadrach Judah…upon his request, of course."

"Mr. Tandy, if you are telling me you murdered," I started when he cut me off with another wave of his slender hand.

"It was Mr. Reuben's request, my dear fellow…I think he would have lived forever had he not gotten sick. Pneumonia, you see. He caught it in that damp and dreadful place and was drowning in his own fluids. Mr. Reuben did not want to die like that. Hard men live and die such hard lives."

"How did you?" I started.

"Simple planning and logistics, Martin…Mr. Reuben wanted a mere three days to put things in order, his will and any loose ends that may have needed taken care of. I worked the late shift back then. So, on October 31st, 1955 just before I started my normal midnight duties, I slipped into room 13A where I administered to inmate, Luther Eli Cobb …a lethal dose of Morphine. I stayed with him beyond the end of my shift and cleaned his body before I escorted it to the crematorium. The final remains of Reuben Shadrach Judah, his military medals and all personal effects, other than the journal of his life were incinerated on November 1st 1955. I remember it was a crisp fall day, cloudless with a bright and heatless sun, a cool breeze coming of the ocean moving inland. In accordance with his will, I took the remains of Mr. Reuben to the high mountains along the Pacific coast and let the Santa Ana winds carry his ashes eastward…to his home. I was only 23 back then," Paul said and closed his eyes. "I was so young…I never knew how many hard miles I had yet to face."

"Did Reuben say anything…any last words?" I asked getting his drugged mind back onto the subject. Paul Tandy opened his eyes and tried to smile, his waxen lips stretched tight like wet paper.

"Odd that you ask, he did ask for a few minutes before I injected the drug into his IV. Mr. Reuben closed his eyes and told me to do what I had to do once he nodded his head…he never once opened his eyes, he only thought for a few brief moments and then Mr. Reuben did something I have never seen him do…he smiled and said five final words before he nodded his head. I administered the drug and Mr. Reuben kept that smile on his face until he stopped breathing."

"What were Reuben's final words?"

"He whispered…the irony of it all. I do not know where Mr. Reuben was when his eyes were closed and he spoke those words, but it is the only time I ever saw him smile. I hope he is now in some far away place where that smile occurred."

"Mr. Reuben is the one who paid for this, isn't he?" I asked. Paul Tandy stared up at me, eyes suddenly sharp.

"Like I said, Martin. I made powerful friends and I took care of them…so they took care of me."

"Are you sure what you have told me is the absolute truth, Paul?"

"Every word dear fellow...every word," he answered and took a raspy breath. "I am so dreadfully tired, so tired...tired of it all."

"I'll come back tomorrow and we can finish up, Paul. I think you need to rest and if my questions have upset you in any way, please forgive me," I apologized. He dismissed the apology with a toss of his hand.

"You have not asked me about the book, Martin." Paul Tandy's eyes were closed again, but a curt smile twisted the corners of his mouth.

"We can talk about the journal Reuben wrote tomorrow after you've rested," I replied, but he knew I was lying. I was hooked with the story, and I desperately wanted that book. It was the only reason I was here.

"You didn't think I knew so much about The Prophet of Cobb Hollow, did you? Mr. Reuben never offered so I never asked about reading his book. Besides, I never possessed the desire to read a solitary page."

"Why?"

"Mr. Reuben would write off and on all night long, he never really slept like other people...I always knew when Mr. Reuben finished another story because he would sit by the window and tell me about his life. He always looked outside when the story was being told and never once looked in my direction nor acknowledged I was there...It was almost like he was back in that certain place reliving that specific day so long ago. Mr. Reuben had a marvelous memory and he possessed the most poetic way of describing mankind's fragilities."

"Really….Interesting," I said, the excitement showing in my voice. The stimulated tone of my reply did not escape Paul Tandy.

"You know, Martin…before I came to care for Mr. Reuben another young man eager to make his literary mark in the world came for the book. Poor fellow underestimated Mr. Reuben's harsh code of moral ethics and found himself cast out of the Prophet's favor."

"I know something about that, Paul. The reporter committed suicide by jumping from a building, didn't he?"

"As a matter of fact he did, jumped from the window of Reuben Judah's room to be exact." Paul Tandy chuckled weakly and then whispered, "Tomorrow the book will be waiting on my bed side table for you, dear fellow."

"Okay, Paul." I wrote the phone number of my hotel room down and turned to leave when his small voice stopped me.

"Before I forget…this may as well go with the book." Paul Tandy opened his gown and removed a thick chain from around his wasted neck. He held out the necklace and let it slide like Eden's forbidden serpent into my hand, metal still warm from his pale and gothic flesh. "The book will be yours tomorrow, goodnight."

I walked into the hallway looking at the chain and the dark and blackened cross clutched to it by a clawed clasp. I rubbed the cross with my thumb and the years of soot disappeared leaving a thin stain on my finger like a burnt and holy avatar. Bright yellow wire gleamed beneath the blackened crust and I realized then that both the cross and chain were solid gold.

****

I was in my hotel room looking out over the bay, watching the sun resurrect itself from the awakening horizon and thinking about Paul Tandy when the phone rang.

"Hello?"

"Is this Martin Carlson?" a sterile voice inquired.

"It is and may I ask who is calling."

"This is the Meadowland Hospice Facility and I am sorry to inform you that Mr. Tandy has passed during the night. I know you are not a relative but a box of personal items was left on his table with your name and this phone number written on it. It will be made available for your procurement at the front reception desk."

I felt only the vain sympathy of knowing that Paul Tandy's suffering had finally ended. "Thank you for calling, I'll be there shortly."

"You're welcome, and I am sorry for your loss."

I dressed and called Simon Archer to explain I would require an extra two days to read the manuscript and rough out an article for the magazine. Simon gave me the authorization before interrogating me about the manuscript of Reuben Judah.

"Is it good?" Simon asked.

"I'm on my way to pick up the manuscript now, I haven't had a chance to read it and that's why I wanted the extra two days to look it over. But from what I have already been told by Paul Tandy, it's going to be good…real good, Simon."

"Alright, go get it and give me a call once you've had a chance to get a feel for the story."

"I will, Simon."

"Good…and one other thing, Martin."

"What's that?"

"It's Saturday and the next time you call me on a weekend remember there's a time zone difference," he said in a smug tone and hung up before I could answer.

I caught a cab and made the trip to Meadowland and back to the hotel in less than thirty minutes, curbing my curiosity and waiting until I was alone in my room before I opened the box Paul Tandy had left. The book was carefully wrapped in a large rack of brown butcher's paper and was the approximate size of a family bible—another smaller box was covered in decorative paper with an envelope attached to the outside. I opened and read the attached letter:

My Dear Martin,

It is with great regret that I must put my last words to prose as I fear the pulling tides of death now guides me to shores elsewhere.

Please care for Mr. Reuben's book as I admired and loved the man greatly. Take caution with what you may discover, for I fear Mr. Reuben's words are far more reaching than his deeds themselves. Sometimes lives are sacrificed so fortunes can be made, but from within the discovery of our mortality...we all die broken and alone.

I would like you to accept the other enclosed item as a gift from myself and Mr. Reuben. Forgive my deceit but as I told you, I have my own connections and I knew more about you before your arrival than you could have possibly known about me. I believe this particular brand of scotch is among the rarest and one that you have coveted fiercely. Please enjoy and I bid you a safe and prosperous journey on life's trouble waters my friend. Remember dear fellow, never let greed guide the soul or fate shall become an inescapable reality.

Best,

Paul Tandy

I opened the slender box and pulled out a bottle of Royal Brackla single malt scotch, aged for 60 years that alone made this bottle one of the rarest vintages of scotch on earth. It was Paul Tandy's final jest, to prove to me and the world that he had the secret friends he seemed so proud of. I opened the sterile paper covering the book then poured three stiff fingers of scotch into a tumbler...I opened Reuben Judah's book to the first page that held the last words written by his hand then toasted Paul Tandy and the secret discretions he had taken to his grave.

San Francisco

October 31ˢᵗ, 1955

Last Will and Testament of Luther Eli Cobb

It is this final oddity of my life and the unknown gambles I have wagered that I now find myself writing the end of my story. I have come to understand that a man is born but his reputation is earned, that it matures through the years as the inescapable chains which bind him to the acoustic shadow of his past deeds. And it is the beguiled character of such validity that will live long after the feebleness of his life and the bread of his table has subsided. Whether or not I am perceived as a just man I cannot say, no person can control the course or opinions of others. And what human truths should be whispered of me shall fade beyond that veracity to leave but a scar of half-legends in the wake of my death. Whether I am right or wrong, believed or not, and beyond that of my scarred flesh I leave only my words and the cross I have bore as both blessing and curse. Only my male attendant, Paul Arthur Tandy shall be permitted to attend my body, I shall be cleaned a final time and then face the flames of cremation. I have come to accept my choice to fan the fires now rather than face the Hell of my eternity later. Know that my ashes are to be spread upon the Santa Ana winds so they may be carried eastward to my home, on those reeking winds of faded wars I will live forever. My ashes will infect the blood of this reawakening land and infuse the bones of all things whether hallowed or hated. Beware to those who would seek to gain fame or profit from the burden of my tale, I am as I am and my revenge will become what you fear most. These are my final words as they are so written by my hand.

My name is Reuben Shadrach Judah, also know as Luther Eli Cobb…and I am the Prophet of Cobb Hollow.

RSJ

First Lifetime

The Quickening

I have endured and survived the hardships of three separate lifetimes. It has become an unbearable affliction. I never asked for war, war came to my doorstep with the false promise of peace. So many years of killing because of it…each death forever stitched into the reflection of a silence and solitude beyond my reach. The divine providence of youth has faded and I now stand in the shadow of my warring sun. I have outlived everything and there is none alive who will object to this final discord of consequences.

My story is complete and I now put the Prophet of Cobb Hollow to rest…it is time.

October 31st 1955

11:55pm.

Reuben Shadrach Judah

The Prophet of Cobb Hollow

****

California State Mental Institution

San Francisco

Alpha Block, Ward Thirteen

The First Night: Monastery of mad Monks

There are such wretched creatures in this place, poor souls who are forced to relive the eternity of some life altering enterprise. They each walked the fine line of conflict in their dismal lives until they lost their balance. Some slight weight shift in the mediocrity of life that tipped the scales to some insane finality—jilted lovers with scarred wrists or those who hid their unchecked and jaded addictions, perhaps some horrible accident thrust them here among the elderly who forever reside within the matrimony of their colliding worlds. Each of them slipped and fell upon the razor's edge, the thread of their obsessive life too fragile and the dynamics of their halved and unbalanced world is now altered forever.

I am solitary among these tortured and desolate characters, condemned to be preyed upon by either the uncaring staff or those inmates among us convicted of sub-human molestations. The time for change has now come upon this place.

May 4th 1939

2:07am

RSJ

****

I will never leave this sanctuary of sorrows alive. Who is to blame, the inmates or the rusted and ruined bars that guard the desperate thoughts of madmen from escaping this forgotten asylum? Would a tree place liability with the nail or the hammer when that first strike impales its grainy surface, altering its flesh forever? Who faults the carpenter?

I have nothing but time to ponder the anti-blessings of my life. Macbeth spoke the truth: *"Tomorrow, and tomorrow, and tomorrow, creeps in this petty place from day to day until the last syllable of recorded time."*

While I wait for one of these abusers of women and children to offer my ancient flesh another scalded scar from the cross—I shall pass my leisure setting fact from fiction. With the scribed words I now put to paper, I so swear this story shall be the truth as I have lived it. My memory is perfect. I will attempt to create a tale of simplicity and lend a quiet validity to the madness that has created my legend…

May 13th 1939

2:33am

RSJ

****

Writing while living with a perfect memory is a curse. The scalded cross has served only as the object to stimulate my past recollections, a tribute to the retributions I have waged.

I have fought in three wars and countless other conflicts and I can still taste the blood, how bitter the venom of its bite. The slow poison working its mental magic forever. I have seen men kill their countrymen to save a stubborn and patriotic nation from itself, witnessed bravery by soldiers whose names are unknown to the written histories of man, and I have traveled to distant lands to face a multitude of brutal conflicts.

I have forged my life upon the dark anvil of war and let those damaged memories crucify me like some vengeful prophet seeking martyrdom. Where is the smell of death more erotic and intoxicating than on the field of battle, where you lose something within yourself and become hopelessly shackled to the nimbus of war's ultimate stimulation? Where else can you feel the violent arch of that passionate trespass?

The shared rapture of that fierce and aggressive conception is thicker than the violent womb of its creation, and only those men who have survived the harsh stratagem of that conflict will understand how true those words ring. Conflict is balance. The invisible line between good and evil…It forces you to choose.

Every man sees themselves as the ultimate warrior in life, but only the 1% will step into the arena and face the divine certainty of death. So many years I have lived a life built upon that creed. So many paths traveled but never once did I face a crossroad. Just a straight line from there to here with nothing but scorched imagery between those inflective points of time.

I am a gladiatorial library of external and internal variances, the oldest living human being on earth … a living pariah. Follow me into the dark well and take the cool drink. It will not last long.

June 13th 1939
1:29am
RSJ

****

To see death is to know that throughout the history of human conflict, after the dead are buried the living bear those silent scars. I remember one summer day as I picked my way through Orange County, Virginia a few months after the Wilderness Battle. I came unaware upon a silent meadow of death and what an appalling spectacle it was. In the cover of red clover laid the unburied remains of soldiers—skeletons side by side almost touching each other like the joined cheeks of long dead lovers. Confederate and Union skulls met skulls, bleached white with those grim and deadly faces still stitched to the very expression of their macabre destruction. Now and then, all war veterans will relive their battles and the brave days of nameless men. They shall recall with great solidarity those ghostly brothers who lay beneath cold stones. Old warriors take new courage from those shrines of great sorrow. Those who are untested in the ways of war venture into these fields of the stony dead and see only the monuments, but the men who fought on that hallowed ground still see with great clarity where bones of the dead once littered the scorched earth, reminders of what evil the men of this world can do.

I once traveled through the war ravaged town of Winchester on a cold night in December (1864), the stars along those blue mountain ridgelines crisp as silver apples dangling from the night sky, passionate buttons of the blind and muted Gods. The windows in that small shanty town were alight by a solitary candle to mark the loss of a soldier, like gold stars each wink of flame a flickering symbol of the heartache that stained the very cusp of this sleeping community. One house near the end of town had four candles burning...and the significance of that Mother's sacrifice did not go unnoticed. The Queen of Angels surely wept because the depth of that burning sorrow had no known length to those candlewicks, no toll for a parent's absolute resolution to such a sudden and excessive forfeit.

If there is a God in some aft and gilded Heaven, I would like to face him ...to have him come down from his thorny throne and answer my simple question. Why war? Why put the curse of destruction within the very marrow of man? I would be ever curious as to the answer.

July 5th, 1939
3:31am
RSJ

******

About the Author

"Mingo Kane was born and raised in Virginia's Blue Ridge Mountains. After high school he entered the United States Army and served with Bravo Company 1st/75th (Airborne) Rangers. Mingo has since enjoyed a host of different and often unique occupations: Bouncer, Security Specialist, first class high voltage lineman and now a full time writer.

When he's not writing Mingo can be found hunting and trapping the mountains near his cabin or on one of the many waterways fly fishing.

Visit Mingo Kane on his Facebook page."

That's the official biography. What you find on the social sites and Amazon. Mingo Kane is far more than that, but he will never tell you. Why?

It's actually really simple: he's a man of honor, honesty, integrity, and humility. He doesn't just represent the 7 Army Values that all soldiers embrace. He is a Ranger who answers to a higher law, and he honors that.

Mingo Kane isn't just someone who cares about his fellow veterans. He cares about everyone. If his kindness, gentleness, and sensitivity to others, his willingness to lend an ear or lend a hand isn't legendary, it should be. Always one with a ready smile, and a kind word, Mingo is the kind of guy that makes you feel you are the only person in the world, and he is there to help you.

In his eyes that armor is tarnished, but underneath all that is a heart of gold that beats for others. He is the Ranger, the Warrior, the Sentinel you are always glad is on watch, and he is always there.

He represents the old slogan "God made Rangers so that Marines would have a hero." And so, much like the main characters in his books, he is always ready to wage war on the side of justice although more often than not, he stands in the shadows, watching, waiting, a true warrior in control of the situation and in control of his life.

Like the Phoenix, another shadow warrior, he is my hero. He is proud of being a Ranger, and they should be proud of having had him among their ranks. He represents not only the Warrior Ethos but the Ranger Creed.

Warrior Ethos
I will always place the mission first.
I will never accept defeat.
I will never quit.
I will never leave a fallen comrade.

Ranger Creed
Recognizing that I volunteered as a Ranger, fully knowing the hazards of my chosen profession, I will always endeavor to uphold the prestige, honor, and high esprit de corps of the Rangers.

Acknowledging the fact that a Ranger is a more elite Soldier who arrives at the cutting edge of battle by land, sea, or air, I accept the fact that as a Ranger my country expects me to move further, faster and fight harder than any other Soldier.

Never shall I fail my comrades. I will always keep myself mentally alert, physically strong and morally straight and I will shoulder more than my share of the task whatever it may be, one-hundred-percent and then some.

Gallantly will I show the world that I am a specially selected and well-trained Soldier. My courtesy to superior officers, neatness of dress and care of equipment shall set the example for others to follow.

Energetically will I meet the enemies of my country. I shall defeat them on the field of battle for I am better trained and will fight with all my might. Surrender is not a Ranger word. I will never leave a fallen comrade to fall into the hands of the enemy and under no circumstances will I ever embarrass my country.

Readily will I display the intestinal fortitude required to fight on to the Ranger objective and complete the mission though I be the lone survivor.

Rangers lead the way!

And there you have it. Mingo Kane is leading the way. This time not as a Ranger but as a skilled writer who writes literary fiction that will draw you in and introduce you to characters you will never forget, plots that make the ordinary extraordinary, and a mastery of the language that makes you laugh, cry, and feel better for having read his work.

Juliet-Juliet